More Favorites by
CHRIS GRABENSTEIN

Escape from Mr. Lemoncello's Library
Mr. Lemoncello's Library Olympics
The Island of Dr. Libris
Welcome to Wonderland: Home Sweet Motel

THE HAUNTED MYSTERY SERIES

COAUTHORED WITH JAMES PATTERSON
Daniel X: Armageddon
Daniel X: Lights Out
House of Robots
House of Robots: Robots Go Wild!
House of Robots: Robot Revolution
I Funny
I Even Funnier
I Totally Funniest
I Funny TV
I Funny: School of Laughs
Jacky Ha-Ha
Treasure Hunters
Treasure Hunters: Danger Down the Nile
Treasure Hunters: Secret of the Forbidden City
Treasure Hunters: Peril at the Top of the World
Word of Mouse

Beach Party Surf Monkey

• Book 2 •

CHRIS GRABENSTEIN

illustrated by Brooke Allen

Random House 🏠 New York

Text copyright © 2017 by Chris Grabenstein
Jacket art and interior illustrations copyright © 2017 by Brooke Allen

Visit us on the Web! randomhousekids.com

Educators and librarians, for a variety of teaching tools, visit us at
RHTeachersLibrarians.com

Library of Congress Cataloging-in-Publication Data
Names: Grabenstein, Chris, author. | Allen, Brooke A., illustrator.
Title: Beach party surf monkey / by Chris Grabenstein ;
illustrations by Brooke Allen.
Description: First edition. | New York : Random House, [2017] |
Series: Welcome to Wonderland ; #2 | Summary: "P.T. and Gloria
try to save the Wonderland again by getting a teen singing sensation
to shoot a movie at the motel" —Provided by publisher.
Identifiers: LCCN 2016014007 | ISBN 978-0-553-53610-2 (hardcover) |
ISBN 978-0-553-53611-9 (hardcover library binding) |
ISBN 978-0-553-53612-6 (ebook)
Subjects: | CYAC: Hotels, motels, etc.—Fiction. |
Motion pictures—Production and direction—Fiction.
Classification: LCC PZ7.G7487 Be 2017 | DDC [Fic]—dc23

Printed in the United States of America
10 9 8 7 6 5 4 3 2 1
First Edition

For Shana Corey,
My *Wonder*ful Editor

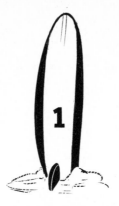

Scary Tales

"**W**hen you live in a motel," I told my audience, "you never know when your neighbors might be fiendish jewel thieves!"

Like always, the whole cafeteria was hanging on my every word. Even the lunch ladies in their plastic shower caps had come out to hear what I'd say next. It was so quiet you could hear a straw squeak its way into a milk carton.

"'Was it dangerous?' you ask. Of course it was! Was I afraid? Ha! Never!"

"How about when the tiger roared?" said my friend Gloria Ortega. "You looked pretty scared then."

I ignored her and kept going.

(That's one of the best things about being a storyteller. You don't have to put in *all* the details.)

"So there we were," I said, "me and Gloria, tailing the two most wanted men in all of Florida."

"The notorious Sneemer brothers!" added Gloria. "From Miami!"

"But we weren't after the two thieves," I said. "Oh, no. We wanted the jewels they'd stolen from the Miami Palm Tree Hotel. Diamonds! Emeralds! Rubies! Cubic zirconias!"

"That's not really a jewel," whispered Gloria.

"Whatever," I whispered back.

And then I amped it up for my big finish, which, by the way, is the most important part of any story. "That's where the race is won," Grandpa always says. "At the finish line!"

It was time to give it everything I had.

"We tracked those two banditos all the way to Tampa International Airport, where we saw them check a bag at curbside—an aluminum attaché case with a combination lock! They'd had it handcuffed to their wrists all day long. . . ."

"And they just checked it at curbside?" asked Pinky Nelligan, one of my best buds, which means he should know better than to ask logical questions while I'm busy making stuff up.

"It was their big mistake," I told him. "Every crook makes one. Some return to the scene of the crime. Some brag to the wrong people. Some check their loot with a baggage handler when they should've kept it chained to their wrists!"

Pinky nodded. So did everybody else.

"Anyway, Gloria and I saw the airline baggage handler put the metal briefcase on a cart."

Gloria gave me a "We did?" look.

It didn't slow me down.

"We chased that cart into the terminal, where another airline worker tossed the briefcase onto a conveyor belt. It disappeared behind some black rubber flaps. So I jumped onto the conveyor belt, too!"

"Didn't the security guards stop you?" asked Kate Mackenzie Williams.

"Oh, they tried," I said with a grin. "But I'm slippery when I want to be. I wasn't going to let them catch me! Even though it meant I might end up in the cargo hold of a jumbo jet headed to Timbuktu!"

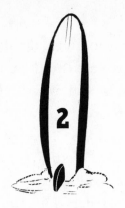

Story Time

"**S**o did you catch up with the briefcase?" asked Kate.

"Oh, yeah," I said. "I followed it all the way out to the runway, where these two big dudes were loading up a plane. They wondered what I was doing riding on a conveyor belt with a bunch of suitcases. I told them I was a bounty hunter following a tip."

"And they believed you?"

"They did when I showed them my badge."

I flashed a tin sheriff's deputy star, which has been crammed inside my wallet since forever. My grandpa used to give the badges away at our motel, the Wonderland, back when he had a ride-along train that looped through the parking lot. Masked actors pretending to be bandits regularly attacked it. Grandpa needed lots of deputies. I have a ton of badges.

"The baggage handlers believed me even more when I popped open that aluminum attaché case and showed them all the hot rocks."

"You mean that candy that explodes in your mouth?" said Kate.

"No," I said. "Those are Pop Rocks."

"'Hot rocks' is what cops call stolen jewelry," said Pinky. "Right, P.T.?"

"Yep."

"What about the jewel thieves?" asked Kate. "What happened to them?"

I shrugged. "Like I said, Gloria and I weren't after the outlaws. We just wanted to return those precious family heirlooms to their rightful owners."

"And pick up the reward money from the insurance company," added Pinky.

"Oh, yeah. That, too!"

"Was it a million-dollar reward?" asked Kate.

"Due to the terms of our settlement," said Gloria, who's an incredible business wiz and knows how to talk like a lawyer when she has to, "we are not at liberty to divulge the exact amount."

"That means we can't tell you how much cash we scored," I told the crowd. "But today, ladies and gentlemen, the Nutty Buddies and ice-cream sandwiches are on us!"

"Woo-hoo!"

Everybody except Gloria and me streamed back to the cafeteria line to grab an ice-cream treat. We strolled outside to meet her dad in front of the school.

Gloria and Mr. Ortega are "extended stay" guests at my family's motel on St. Pete Beach because Mr. Ortega recently landed a job as a sports reporter on WTSP, our local CBS station.

"He's working his way up the dial" is how Gloria puts it. "Hopping from one station to the next, moving from city to city, hoping to one day land his dream job at ESPN."

"ESPN is the leader of the pack," Mr. Ortega tells me all the time. "And if you're not running with the lead dogs, P.T., all you see is a bunch of furry butts."

Anyway, right after the news broke that "Two Florida kids solve decades-old jewel heist," all sorts of TV and radio people wanted to interview me and Gloria. Well, mostly me. Gloria "doesn't do" TV.

"That's Dad's wheelhouse," she says.

I had no idea what manning the wheel of a boat had to do with being on TV, but I agreed to handle all the press requests—including the call from *Everyday Superstars,* a show on ESPN5 that airs at like three in the morning . . . every other Tuesday.

I told them I'd do it—but only if Manny Ortega (that's Mr. Ortega's TV name) did the interview.

I wanted to help him run with the big dogs.

Hey, he's a good guy. He should look at stuff besides furry dog butts.

More Famous Than Amos!

"I am standing with P. T. Wilkie, the boy who cracked the fabled Miami Palm Tree Hotel jewel heist case," Mr. Ortega told the camera lens. "And, sports fans, you can just feel the electricity in the air."

Gloria's dad was dressed in a snazzy blue blazer with an ESPN5 patch stitched to the chest pocket. As always, he looked extremely handsome, with every strand of his shiny hair pastéd into place. His smile was brighter than the TV lights blinding me. His eyes twinkled almost as much as his teeth.

"Up against the infamous Sneemer brothers," Mr. Ortega continued, "young P.T. brought his A game. He left it all out on the field. He knew what he had to do and went out there and did it."

Because he wants to be on ESPN, Mr. Ortega knows a ton of sportscaster clichés and he's not afraid to use them.

"By the way," I said, "we're celebrating the rescue of the stolen jewels this coming Saturday with special guided tours at the Wonderland Motel, 7000 Gulf Boulevard, where there are always marvels to behold and stories to be told. All T-shirts are buy one, get one free, this weekend only. Limit two per customer. Void where prohibited."

Before I left for school that morning, Grandpa reminded me to plug our newest attraction. He's the one who opened Walt Wilkie's Wonder World way back in October 1970. That's right. Exactly one year before that other Walt opened Disney World over in Orlando.

"We had a very good year, P.T.," Grandpa always tells me. "A very good year."

Now the Wonderland is mostly an old-school motel with lots of wacky statues (we have a giant dinosaur *and* a bucking jackalope) decorating the property. Between the reward money that helped us pay off what bankers call a "balloon loan" (it's a mortgage, not a loan to buy balloons) and the hype around the jewel heist and the notorious thieves who'd stayed in rooms 103 and 114, we had a shot at another very good year. Maybe two!

"By finding those stolen jewels," said Mr. Ortega in his smoothest broadcaster voice, "you, P. T. Wilkie, have become the most famous, most beloved middle school student in the entire state of Florida. How does that make you feel?"

"Awesome!"

Mr. Ortega nodded and smiled. "As it should. But be mindful of what a great football coach once said: 'Success is about having; excellence is about being.'"

"Huh?" I was confused. Mr. Ortega was starting to sound like Yoda from the *Star Wars* movies.

He turned to the camera to tell the whole world what he and the coach had meant.

"Some think success is all about having money and fame. But excellence, my friends, is about being the best *you* that you can possibly be! From Ponce de León Middle School in St. Petersburg, Florida, this is Manny Ortega." He fist-thumped the chest patch on his blazer. "For ESPN-Five."

I still didn't totally get what Mr. Ortega had been talking about. But to tell you the truth, I didn't really care.

I was on TV.

I was famous!

Mr. Grumpface

After the interview, Gloria and I headed to grumpy Mr. Frumpkes's class.

Yes, everybody calls him Mr. Grumpface. Even the other teachers.

If the Ponce de León yearbook had pages for "Least Favorite Teacher" and "Most Likely to Annoy," Mr. Frumpkes's photo would be on both. Every year.

Francis Frumpkes

No, I will not say "cheese."

Most Likely Not to Smile at Puppies

Cheese is nothing but curdled mold made out of rancid dairy products.

Mr. Frumpkes teaches history, or, as I like to call it, the Study of Famous Dead People.

"You're tardy, Mr. Wilkie," Mr. Frumpkes said when Gloria and I hurried into his classroom five minutes after the second bell.

"Sorry," I said. "We had this TV thing."

Mr. Frumpkes made like he was playing the world's tiniest violin with his thumbs and forefingers.

"Oh, dear," he said sarcastically. "A TV thing. My heart weeps for you, Mr. Wilkie."

"I guess I was tardy, too," said Gloria.

"No, Miss Ortega. You were simply associating with the wrong individual. I know you're new here at Ponce de León, but you should really try to cultivate a better caliber of friend."

"But, sir," said Gloria, "isn't the freedom of assembly, and, therefore, the right to associate with whomever I choose, guaranteed to all American citizens under the First Amendment to the United States Constitution?"

Mr. Frumpkes's ears turned purple. It looked like he was wearing eggplants for earmuffs.

"This is Ponce de León Middle School, Miss Ortega—not the United States of America. Sit down, both of you, before I remember where I put my pink detention pad!"

Gloria and I did as we were told. We were both too busy after school coming up with new business schemes to keep the Wonderland running in the black (that's how Gloria says "making money") to waste time sitting in detention hall.

Mr. Frumpkes clasped his hands behind his back and paced at the front of the room.

"Now then, where was I? Ah, yes. The Big Lie. History's time-honored propaganda technique. People will always fall for a big lie over a small one. For instance, today in the cafeteria, a certain student told a *huge* whopper, claiming he had heroically thwarted a pair of jewel thieves by jumping onto a baggage carousel at the Tampa airport."

He brandished a copy of the *Tampa Bay Times*.

"The truth of the matter is, I'm afraid, somewhat less dramatic."

"So?" said Pinky. "The story gets better every time P.T. tells it!"

"Next time," added Kate, "maybe Kevin the Monkey will be in it!"

"Oooh!" said the whole class. "Kevin! The Monkey!"

"And who, pray tell, is Kevin the Monkey?" asked Mr. Frumpkes. "One of your pimple-faced pop stars?"

"Kevin the Monkey is a supercool capuchin from the Sunshine State Primate Sanctuary," said Kate. "He's a total YouTube sensation!"

"And a savvy PR vehicle," added Gloria. "Last year, Kevin the Monkey's channel earned one point six million dollars for the animal rescue charity, thanks to rollover ads. Net-net, he and the primate sanctuary have put together a rock-solid monkey business plan!"

When Gloria said that, the class cracked up.

"Monkey business!"

The laughter grew louder when somebody (probably Kate Mackenzie Williams, because she's a total gadget freak) used their phone to hack into the Smart Board's Wi-Fi connection and run a hysterical Kevin the Monkey clip.

I figured it was a good thing Mr. Frumpkes couldn't find his detention pad.

Otherwise, the whole class would be doing hard time after school.

Home Sweet Motel

When Gloria and I walked home to the Wonderland after school, a car nearly cut us off while pulling into the humongous parking lot of the Conch Reef Resort, our brand-new next-door neighbor.

There used to be three other small family-run motels south of us: the Flamingo, the Sand Castle, and the Treasure Aire.

Now there was a fourteen-story concrete monstrosity with a ginormous plasma-screen reader board out front reminding everybody that they could eat all the "World-Famous Grouper Fingers with Tartar Sauce" they wanted for $5.99 during the Conch Reef Restaurant's early-bird dinner special.

We don't have an early-bird dinner special at the Wonderland.

We don't even have a restaurant.

"Catch you later, P.T.," said Gloria as she clomped up the staircase to her room on the second floor.

"Later."

"Hang on," she called from the balcony. "Dad just texted. UPS delivered the candy necklaces, jawbreaker bracelets, and gummy bear earrings. I need to start packaging souvenirs for Saturday's tours."

"What's our cost of goods?" I asked. Gloria and I sometimes watch a TV show called *Shark Tank* together on Friday nights, and those billionaires are always asking people about the cost of goods.

"Fifty cents," said Gloria. "We'll mark up each S-K-U five hundred percent, to three dollars, for a gross profit margin of eighty-three percent."

"Cool," I said. "Um, what's an S-K-U?"

"We call 'em 'skews,'" said Gloria. "It's short for stock-keeping unit."

Fact: it is awesome being in business with Gloria Ortega.

I went into the lobby (my mom and I live in rooms 101 and 102, behind the front desk), and right away a group of tourists wanted my autograph.

"You're the boy!" said a lady.

"The kid who recovered all those stolen jewels!" said a man.

Both were wearing the souvenir "Jewel Thieves Slept Here" T-shirts Gloria had dreamed up. (For sale in the Wonderland lobby for $19.99. Available in infant and toddler sizes, too.)

"Can you autograph our shirts?" asked the lady.

"Sure," I said, whipping out the marker I always carry in one of the flapped pockets of my cargo shorts. It was beyond awesome to be a celebrity in my own home.

But the real reason I love all this sudden fame? My dad.

As you may have noticed, he's not really in the picture. Actually, he's not in *any* pictures I've ever seen. I don't even know what the guy looks like.

"Where is he?" you ask. Well, I'd usually answer that kind of question by making up another quick story—one with such a dazzling, pie-in-face opening hook that you'd be too blown away to wonder if what I was saying was true. You know, something like "He's not here because the CIA needs him up in Canada."

"There's trouble in Canada?" you'd say.

"Nope," I'd tell you. "But only because my dad's been stationed there for a dozen years on an international peacekeeping mission. If he came home? Watch out. There could be a sticky maple syrup war."

The truth? I don't really know where my dad is or what he's doing. But I'm guessing that when he finds out his son is the most famous middle school student in Florida, that I'm a certified celebrity, he'll fly down here to meet me just as fast as he can!

Even if it means the start of a messy maple syrup war.

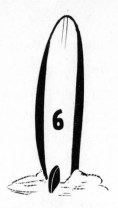

Freebies

The tourists left with their autographed T-shirts.

I went to the soda machine and bopped it in the sweet spot. Down plunked a cold can of orange soda.

My mom came out of the office just as my drink *ka-thunk*ed into the slot.

"P.T.?"

Fact: I was busted.

"I told you, hon—no more freebies from the vending machines."

"But we don't have to worry about money anymore. We paid off the bank loan. Business is booming. The 'No' is lit on the vacancy sign."

"And we're still barely making ends meet. Look, I appreciate all that you, Gloria, and your grandpa have done, but—"

Tiny bells jingled.

"But what?" Grandpa walked into the lobby.

Mom sighed. She does that a lot when she's not nibbling pen tips or crunching numbers on her calculator.

"But what, Wanda?" Grandpa repeated.

"We have to be prudent, Dad," said Mom.

"Prudent?" said Grandpa. "Baaaah." He swatted at the air. "I never did like that word. *Prudent.* Reminds me of prunes. *Dented* prunes. And prunes make me go to the bathroom!"

Grandpa bopped the soda machine in the sweet spot. (He's the one who taught me where it is.) Down dropped a free can of his favorite beverage: Dr. Brown's Cel-Ray soda. Yep. It tastes like a gassy version of those celery sticks nobody eats when they order buffalo wings.

"P.T.," said Grandpa when his burp was finally finished, "I've been thinking. How would you and Gloria like to be my new train robbers when I get the Wonderland Express up and running again? Your pal Pinky can be my new sheriff. He's got the face for it. Handsome. Honest. Dimpled chin."

"I don't know," I said jokingly. "I still have my deputy badge from back in the day. It might be against the rules for me to switch sides and join the bad guys."

"Rules, schmules. I'll give you both red-checkered kerchiefs you can use as masks—plus cowboy hats *and* silver cap guns you can twirl on your trigger fingers!"

"Deal!"

Mom rolled her eyes and mumbled to herself, "Why am I the only grown-up in this family?"

It's what she mumbles whenever Grandpa has another nutty idea.

Me? I love his crazy schemes almost as much as I love living in this crazy motel. Every room has free cable, tiny bottles of shampoo, and ice buckets with plastic liners. Plus, the pizza joint down the street will deliver right to your room.

It's kid heaven!

The string of bells over the lobby door jingled again.

In walked our new neighbors: Mr. Conch and his daughter, Veronica. I recognized them both from the Conch High-Quality Resorts TV commercials, where he always says, "If it's good enough for my princess, Veronica, trust me, folks—it'll be good enough for you and yours."

Veronica was wearing a school uniform with a plaid wool skirt because she goes to a ritzy private school instead of Ponce de León Middle, like me and Gloria. Her shoes were covered with sparkling red sequins. I'm guessing when she was little, all her Barbie dolls wore diamond tiaras and mink coats.

Mr. Conch was smiling like a shark set loose in a lobster tank.

And I had a feeling we might be the lobsters.

Meet Mr. Conch

"**E**dward!" Grandpa said to the smarmy man with an even smarmier mustache. "Long time no see. Missed you at the last Hospitality Association meeting."

"Been busy, Walt." He shot out his hand for Grandpa to shake it.

"Wanda, P.T.," said Grandpa, "this is our new neighbor Mr. Edward Conch."

Yep. Our new neighbor. Also known as the guy who ordered the bulldozers to demolish our *old* neighbors.

"We're very proud to have opened the Conch Reef Resort condo-beach-resort-restaurant complex next door," said Mr. Conch. "It joins our growing family of the most magnificent high-quality ocean-front resorts, condos, time-sharing properties, and fine-dining establishments up and down the Gulf Coast. At Conch High-Quality Resorts, you always get what you want because I always get what I want!"

Mr. Conch puffed up his chest.

I'm sure if he'd had tail feathers, he would've ruffled those out for us, too.

There was a cloud of cologne swirling around him. My eyes were watering a little. Mr. Conch should probably wear an allergy hazard warning.

"It's a pleasure to finally meet you, Mr. Conch," said Mom.

"I know, Wanda," said Mr. Conch. "People love meeting me. I'd like to meet me, too, but forget about it, that's not gonna happen. I probably should've dropped by sooner, seeing as how all of a sudden we're next-door neighbors, but what can I say, folks? Been busy. We just opened and already business is booming, which is what happens at all Conch High-Quality Resorts. I'm worth what? Two, three billion dollars. Maybe more."

"I thought we were going to get ice cream, Daddy," whined Veronica.

"In a minute, honey. We need to talk to the Wilsons first."

"Wilkies," said Grandpa.

Mr. Conch shrugged. "Right. Whatever. How you doin', son?"

He rubbed my hair like I was one of those hand dryers at the bowling alley.

I hate when people rub my hair. Especially when their hands smell like freshly mowed hay mixed with Chinese fortune cookie crumbs.

"I've heard about you, kid," said Mr. Conch. "Seen you on TV, too. You're Petey, am I right?"

"P.T.," I said. "It's short for Phineas Taylor."

"We named him after P. T. Barnum," said Grandpa.

"Because this kid's a little huckster," Mr. Conch said admiringly. "Jewel thief tour. Two-for-one T-shirt sale. Brilliant, kid. Very impressive. You remind me of me. You're over here running all sorts of scams and cons, making a fast buck, because we both know there's a sucker born every minute, am I right?"

Mom tried to get a word in edgewise. "P.T. and his friends aren't—"

Mr. Conch snapped his fingers. His daughter rolled her eyes and handed Mom a blue tin of those Danish butter cookies nobody really likes.

"These cookies are for you, Ms. Wilkie," she said like a robot programmed to be polite.

"Why, thank you, Veronica."

"Are those butter ring cookies?" asked Grandpa. "I like those. You can stick 'em on your finger and nibble around the edges."

"These are Danish, Walt," said Mr. Conch. "That means they're imported from Daneland. Very high-class. Like I told Veronica, only the best, most exquisite cookies in the world for our new, extremely successful neighbors."

"Well, we have had a good little run lately," said Mom modestly.

"Go figure, huh?" said Mr. Conch. "Your old-fashioned motel with all the gewgaws and very small pool—I'm sorry, it is, it's tiny—your dinky motel is stealing business from my brand-new, luxurious, world-class resort, even though we're right next door. How's that happen? I'll tell you how: your boy Petey here keeps cooking up clever moneymaking schemes, am I right?"

"I can't take all the credit, sir," I said modestly. "It's a team effort."

"Hey, enjoy it while you can. Remember Silly Bandz?"

"No," I admitted.

"Neither does anybody else! That's my point. A few years ago, they were a multibillion-dollar fad. Today? Nobody's ever even heard of them."

"What are you trying to say, Edward?" asked Grandpa.

"Simple. In a month, maybe two, your motel will be yesterday's news. Everybody will move on to the next big thing."

Mr. Conch snapped his fingers again.

His daughter sighed, gave us another eye roll, and handed Grandpa a business card, which he immediately turned over to Mom.

"But imagine if you didn't have to worry about anything ever again," said Mr. Conch.

Mom stared at the business card. I stared at the big blowhard's smug smirk. He looked like he thought he'd just gotten away with a silent fart.

"The all-new Conch Reef Resort is huge," he

continued. "But to be honest, I want it to be huger. I want to expand."

"Already?" said Mom. "You just opened."

"I don't wait for opportunity to knock, Wanda. I like to ring its doorbell. My architects tell me if I had another chunk of adjacent property, I could add a new wing. Put in a lazy river. Kids love a lazy river, what with the inner tubes and the drifting. Maybe we could even add on a high-class spa with those cucumber-and-mud facials. So I thought to myself, 'Hey, Ed, you know what would be brilliant?' 'No, Ed, what?' 'A nice empty lot! Maybe where that Wonderland Motel used to be.'"

"You want to buy our property?" asked Mom. "You want to tear down the Wonderland?"

"No. All I want to do, Wanda, is take away all your cares and worries. Your brow? It's so furrowed you could plant potatoes up there. But you sell out to me? You waltz away with so much cash you could retire and send your son to any state college you want."

"Sell out?" said Grandpa, his voice cracking.

"Do it for my customers, Walt," said Mr. Conch.

"I don't know. . . ."

"Hey, at Conch High-Quality Resorts, the customers always get what they want. You know why? Because I always get what I want."

Putting Lipstick on a Pig

The next morning, as always, Mom and I met Gloria and her dad in the lobby.

It's what the four of us do at the start of every day, before Gloria and I walk to the school bus stop together. We'd already set up the free breakfast buffet—mostly doughnuts, bagels, and a couple of bananas. Oh, and orange juice. This is Florida. I think serving OJ every morning is a state law.

"Would you like a powdered doughnut, Manuel?" Mom asked Mr. Ortega, batting her eyelashes so much they looked like a pair of spiders clapping. She wasn't wearing her glasses, either. She never does when Mr. Ortega is in the room. She'd even stopped surfing the Web, where she'd been checking out retirement villas near Tucson, Arizona, ever since Grandpa had handed her Mr. Conch's business card.

Arizona, unlike Florida, has a "dry heat."

"No thanks, Wanda," said Mr. Ortega. "A banana and a cup of OJ are all I really need to get my motor running."

"Me too," said Mom, putting down the bagel she had already smeared with strawberry-flavored cream cheese.

Fact: when she's near Mr. Ortega, Mom acts like this girl Ava at school who's always gawking at a poster of that teen heartthrob Aidan Tyler she keeps taped up inside her locker.

Double fact: I don't mind. Mr. Ortega is a pretty neat guy. And his smile *is* glisteny.

Gloria and I took off and headed up the sidewalk on our way to the bus stop.

"I did some research," she said. "Conch Enterprises is on a buying binge." Gloria watches nothing but financial news networks on the TV in her room, even though she has 257 channels to choose from.

"What does that mean?" I asked.

"They're looking for rapid expansion opportunities to make their books look better to investors. We call it putting lipstick on a pig. But then again, bulldozing the Wonderland to add square footage to the Conch Reef Resort would be a seamless integration aligning with their core competencies."

As usual, I had no idea what Gloria was talking about. (I sometimes wonder if even she does.)

So I changed the subject.

"Well, we won't have to sell out to Mr. Conch if we keep coming up with spectacular moneymakers like our Jewel Thief Tour. He'd heard about it, Gloria. I think we scare him a little."

"Possible," said Gloria. "Your brain, my business savvy. We make a formidable team."

"Totally. I'll pass out the flyers today during lunch. Drum up a *huge* crowd. Show Mr. Conch that we don't need him or his bulldozers. Is the merchandise department ready to rock?"

"Just about. Dad and I boxed up all the candy jewelry last night."

"Boxes? I thought we were doing plastic bags."

"Wrong brand image, P.T. Bags say 'candy.'

Cotton-lined blue boxes say jewelry. They also say five dollars instead of three. *Boom!* Our profit margins just went through the roof!"

"Boom!" We fist-bumped on it.

"Pinky's all set, too," I told Gloria. "He'll be in the parking lot singing 'The Ballad of the Jewel Thieves' starting at nine o'clock sharp."

"There's a song like that?"

"Yep. I wrote it for him."

"And Pinky can sing?"

"Totally! He's been the lead in the school musicals and a soloist with the church choir since kindergarten. After he fires up the crowd, I step in and lead the first tour at nine-fifteen. We hit all the high points of the jewel thieves hiding out at the motel."

"Slight problem, P.T. I don't remember all that many high points."

"I know. That's why I had to make up a bunch. I drilled a bullet hole in Morty D. Mouse's fiberglass butt."

"Um, the Sneemer brothers didn't have guns. They didn't shoot holes into any of the statues."

"Maybe not. But if they'd had guns, they could've. Oh—Grandpa promised me he'll repaint the Muffler Man statue into a cat burglar while we're at school. This is going to be huge!"

Strumming Up Business

On Saturday morning, our sun-drenched parking lot was packed with cars and people.

Pinky strolled around, plunking the three guitar chords he knows and singing the song I wrote for the grand opening of our Wonderland Jewel Thief Tour.

"Just step right up
And you'll hear a tale,
A tale of gold and jewels.
It took place on this very spot
With two crooks who were fools!"

"First tour starts in fifteen minutes," I announced through my megaphone. "Tickets are just five dollars, ten for VIP privileges."

"What's in the VIP package?" asked a dad herding six kids.

"Exclusive potty breaks. In addition to the public facilities in the lobby, VIPs receive an all-access pass to the bathrooms in rooms 103 and 114, the very same toilets the notorious Sneemer brothers used while they were hiding out here at the motel."

"Seven VIP tickets," said the dad, eagerly handing me seventy bucks. For him, it was probably a bargain. His kids were guzzling juice boxes the way kindergartners do after a soccer game. One already had a leg jiggling in full "I've got to pee" mode.

The juice boxes came from the concession stand, manned by Grandpa.

"Who wants a Cel-Ray soda?" he cried. "Cel-Ray will make your day!"

And then he burped. Good thing nobody was standing too close. They might've keeled over.

"Focus on the juice boxes, Grandpa," I whispered. "And the jewelry cake balls."

Gloria and I invented those. We went to Dunkin' Donuts, picked up a couple dozen Munchkins, and dusted them with silver sugar sprinkles and those tiny silver candy beads they sell in the baking aisle at the supermarket.

Gloria was making major money at her souvenir stand. She was right: the penny candy in the fancy blue boxes was selling like cheap imitation jewelry on the Home Shopping Network (not that I ever watch those kinds of shows). So were the sparkly new "Wonderland: Jewel of St. Pete Beach" T-shirts studded with rhinestones over the two *O*s so they looked like diamond rings.

We were going to clear a couple thousand dollars, easy. If we did this every Saturday, we'd never, *ever* have to sell out to our skeevy next-door neighbor Mr. Conch—the man with the gold-plated wrecking ball.

Mom came out of the office to join me and Grandpa near the concession stand. She had a rolled-up brochure from an Arizona retirement community in her hand. I wanted to tell her, *I'm a kid! I'm too young to retire!*

But I could tell she was still seriously considering selling out to Mr. Conch.

"I don't believe this," she said. "These people are each paying you five dollars to walk around, look at the swimming pool, and check out a couple of the statues? They could do that for free."

"True," I said. "But they wouldn't hear the action-packed story of how we beat the bandits. On the tour, they can thrill to all the chilling details and hear the never-before-told tale of what happened when I warned the Sneemer brothers they couldn't fill up their huge ice chest with free ice from the ice machine."

"What happened?"

"See? Even you're interested! And then I'll show 'em the hole in Morty D. Mouse's fiberglass butt. Were shots fired when the bandits fled on foot, chased by Mad Max, our trusty dog?"

"P.T.?" said Mom. "We don't have a dog."

"I know. That's why I have to say it as if it's a question. That way I'm not lying. This is what English teachers call a tall tale. Only instead of Paul Bunyan and Babe, his big blue ox, we're giving them the Sneemer brothers and Morty, our big gray mouse."

"Relax, Wanda," said Grandpa. "We're a roadside attraction, not a history museum. These folks came here for the old razzle-dazzle."

"And I'm gonna give it to them!"

"Attaboy, P.T.!"

Of course, that was when Mr. Frumpkes, our history teacher, pulled into the parking lot.

And he'd brought his own bullhorn.

Good-bye, Sparkle and Glitter

"**G**ood citizens of St. Petersburg Beach!" cried Mr. Frumpkes through his bullhorn, which was squealing like a sick dolphin. "Visiting tourists! Beware! The story you are about to hear is not true. It is, in fact, fallacious!"

"What do you mean?" asked the dad who'd just given me seventy bucks so his kids could use a jewel thief's potty.

"It's a lie!" Mr. Frumpkes waved a newspaper in the air. "Here's the truth, the whole truth, and nothing but the truth!"

I hate when people say that.

It means everything is about to become super boring. Where's the drama? The suspense? The story?

"That young whippersnapper over there is a

Listen to me, people! I am a **certified** history teacher!

You're a certified stick-in-the-mud, too!

known exaggerator!" Frumpkes declared. "He is an unreliable narrator!"

Mom reached out. Squeezed my hand. The look on her face? She was eyeballing Mr. Frumpkes the way a mama bear eyeballs anybody who gets between her and her cub.

"The stolen jewels were not recovered here at this motel," Mr. Frumpkes blared on. "Hardly! They were found all the way across the bay in Tampa at an animal sanctuary known as Wild Cat Safariland!"

"Maybe so," snapped Gloria. "But the jewel thieves really did stay here. P.T., his grandfather, and I really were the ones who recovered the stolen merchandise!"

"Correct," said Mr. Frumpkes. "Therefore, if you insist on giving tours to celebrate your glorious adventures, Miss Ortega, I suggest you pile these poor people into a bus and do your tour over in Tampa—not down the street from my mother's house! Her mah-jongg group is having trouble finding parking spaces!"

Long story short?

Everybody left.

We refunded all their money.

We also ate jewelry cake pops for lunch. Mom and Mr. Ortega said the candy necklaces, jaw-breaker bracelets, and gummy bear earrings would be our dessert "for the foreseeable future."

Actually, just Mom said that. Then she went back to Googling "good schools in Tucson, Arizona."

Mr. Ortega tried to buck us up with more of his sportscaster lingo.

"Sure, you've got to go back and regroup, maybe circle the wagons, make some adjustments at half-time. But remember, kids, it ain't over till it's over."

"Dad?" said Gloria. "It's over. Everybody left."

Mr. Ortega nodded grimly. "The ball just didn't

bounce our way today, Gloria. We have to put this loss behind us."

Gloria and I spent the rest of our Saturday moping around and hanging out in the lobby with Cheeseball, my cat. I was wondering how Cheeseball would like all that dry heat out in Arizona. If Mom made us move, it might make her fur less frizzy.

"Do you realize," said Gloria, fiddling with a whirring calculator, "this is our first moneymaking venture that actually *lost* money?"

Cheeseball meowed. I think she was trying to cheer us up.

Suddenly, I heard a screech. Cheeseball shot out her claws. They dug through my shorts as she sprang out of my lap.

A car slammed on its brakes. Tires squealed. Horns honked. Someone screamed.

Cheeseball ran under the nearest sofa.

She doesn't like loud, high-pitched noises.

Especially when they sound like a car wreck.

Surprise Guest Star

Gloria and I raced out of the lobby and into the parking lot fronting Gulf Boulevard.

Several large SUVs had skidded to a stop. Guys with cameras jumped out of the big black vehicles to snap pictures and grab videos of a shaggy-haired blond guy in board shorts and white-framed sunglasses who was being chased by a mob of girls.

Now the girls (not the car brakes) were the ones doing all the shrieking and squealing.

"Yo!" Shaggy, who was sort of short, shouted at me, whipping off his shades. "Help me out, man! These girls love me like crazy!"

"Uh, this way," I said, because I could tell he needed help. I grabbed hold of his arm.

"Yo, ease up, Slick. Just got a new tat inked on that arm."

"Sorry."

"Aidan!" somebody shouted behind a clicking camera. "Look this way!"

"Aidan!" shouted a man with a microphone. "What are you doing on St. Pete Beach?"

"Aidan, did you really break up with Dasani so you could date Aisha?" shouted someone else.

"What can I say, man? I love the ladies! All of 'em."

Some girls shrieked some more. Louder. Some guys started shrieking, too. It reminded me of when a flock of seagulls discovers an unguarded sandwich on the beach.

"But please," the guy named Aidan shouted back, "leave Aisha alone! Let our love, like, blossom."

More shrieking. Squealing. One swoon.

The crowd crushed forward.

"Back up, people," said Gloria, standing firmly in her Wonder Woman power pose, which she heard about in some kind of talk on the Internet. She tells me standing like that makes her feel invincible (which, trust me, she totally is). "This parking lot is for the private use and enjoyment of registered guests only."

I hustled the little guy toward the lobby door. As I did, I checked out his golden bangs. Somebody had cut them to look messy but totally neat. He also had these green-green eyes (they sort of reminded me of swamp scum) that I'd seen before. I couldn't remember where until I finally did: inside Ava's locker at school.

The guy in the board shorts was none other than the one and only Aidan Tyler!

As I grabbed the door, I realized that if I took Aidan Tyler into the lobby of the Wonderland, he'd be like a prize blowfish in an aquarium. His fans would just press up against the glass to gawk at him. Some girl would probably make smoochy faces at him, too. And that would mean I'd have to spend my weekend cleaning greasy lipstick smears off our floor-to-ceiling windows.

"Change of plans," I told him.

"That's cool, man. I'm up for whatever."

"Gloria?" I shouted over my shoulder. "I'm going with plan D!"

"Gotcha!" she hollered back, never breaking out of her power pose.

"So, what's plan D?" asked Aidan.

"We hide," I whispered. "Inside a giant dinosaur."

Ducking into a Dinosaur

Dino, our big green fiberglass dinosaur around back, has a secret door in his rump.

Grandpa used to store junk in there—putters

Authorized Personnel ONLY.
This does _not_ mean You.

for the miniature golf course, lawn flamingos, paint cans, old sneakers.

"It was cheaper than buying another shed!" he told me.

Gloria and I have since turned it into our private clubhouse. It's a great place to hang out, swap stories, and plot schemes—except in August. Then it's more like a sauna inside an oven located at the molten core of the earth.

That day, though, it was the perfect hiding place for teen idol Aidan Tyler.

"Here comes Gloria," I said, staring through the periscope we'd rigged up inside Dino's tail. "You'd better stand away from the door."

"Too true," said Aidan, backing up against the curved fiberglass walls, which are kind of bumpy and knobby on the inside of a statue, since, you know, nobody really looks at that part.

I swung the door open. Gloria leapt in. I slammed the door shut and hurried back to the periscope.

"Did they follow me?" Gloria asked breathlessly.

I held my finger to my lips.

We needed to keep quiet.

Through the periscope, I could see a clump of girls tromping around like they were on an Easter egg hunt.

"Aidan? We love you! Aidan? Where are you?"

Aidan slumped to the floor, shaking his head. "It's, like, crazy out there, man."

Gloria motioned for him to remain quiet. Then she gestured to our snack box. It's a cooler we keep loaded with Oreos, cheese balls, kettle corn—the essentials. We would keep soda in there, too, but we're not idiots. Some days it gets so hot inside Dino's rear end, cans explode.

Trust me.

We learned this the hard way.

We did have some bottles of water. And a couple of cartons of warm orange juice because, like I said, in Florida, OJ availability at all times is mandatory.

I passed a bunch of the snacks and a bottle of warmish water over to Aidan Tyler.

"Hey, you guys!" we heard one of the girls holler. "There he is! I think I see Aidan! Down on the beach!"

"SQUEEEEE!"

On the other side of the dinosaur walls, we heard the muffled sounds of a teenaged cattle stampede.

We gave it a few more minutes. Aidan sipped his warm water. Gloria nibbled an Oreo. I rechecked the periscope.

"The coast is clear," I announced. "There's nobody out there except a pelican. No, wait. That's a new statue."

"Let's give the paparazzi out front a few more minutes to pack up their gear," suggested Gloria.

"I can dig it, man," said Aidan.

In case you've been living in a cave (or the butt end of a dinosaur) for a few years, here's the scoop on Aidan Tyler: His concerts always sell out the day tickets go on sale. He's only seventeen and already has a dozen platinum records and millions of lunch boxes with his face and green-green eyes plastered all over them. He's on the cover of *Teen Ink, J-14,* and *Popstar!* magazines all the time and probably spends two hours every day scrunching his hair to make it look perfectly messy. Come to think of it, he's so rich he probably pays someone to scrunch it for him.

"This, like, your motel, man?" Aidan asked me.

"Sort of. My grandpa owns it. My mom runs it."

"Tell you what, dude—because you two, like, rescued me from the mob and because I'm, like, a totally awesome individual, I'm gonna toss your motel's name into the hat."

"Fantastic!" I said. "Um, what hat are we talking about?"

"For my first-ever movie. That's why I'm here in St. Petersburg, F-L-A. We're, like, scouting locations for my upcoming big-screen debut. Competition is off the chain. Every motel, hotel, and resort in Tampa Bay wants the gig. They're pitching my producers tomorrow."

"Quick question," I said, remembering how much money we'd just lost on our Jewel Thief Tour, which tanked even faster than Silly Bandz. "When you shoot a movie at a location, do you, you know, pay?"

"No. I mean I, personally, don't pay for anything anymore, man. I have people who do that kind of stuff for me. I don't even carry coinage in my pocket, just a bundle of Benjamins, because, you know, that's how I roll."

Gloria and I both nodded.

"But the movie company?" said Aidan. "They'll pay you a ton to rent out your place for a few weeks. Plus, if your motel's in my movie, it'll be famous forever, man—just like that hotel where Elvis filmed *Blue Hawaii!*"

"We'll be famous?" I was practically drooling.

"Forever, dude. Just like me."

The Grand Tour?

I knew that Aidan had to meet Grandpa.

When it comes to selling the wonders of the Wonderland, nobody does it better than Walt Wilkie.

If, with Aidan Tyler's help, we could turn our motel into a famous movie location landmark, Mom would forget all about selling out to Mr. Conch and moving to Arizona. Too many people from all over the world would want to visit and stay at the Wonderland once it became a movie star.

So I texted Grandpa:

MEET ME BEHIND DINO!

He, of course, *called* me back.

"P.T.?" he said. "What are these words someone's

typing on my telephone screen here? Why is it all of a sudden making funny squiggly sounds?"

Grandpa's new to smartphones.

"Meet us behind Dino!" I told him.

"Why?"

"We have a very important guest."

"Ohhh. Is it the president?"

"No."

"Then it can wait. I'm eating lunch. Bologna and mustard on white bread with pickle relish. You want one?"

"No thanks. Grandpa? Our guest is a major celebrity and he's looking for a motel to use as the setting for his first movie."

"Ooh. They pay for that."

"I know. And nobody bulldozes down motels once they've been in a movie. Hurry!"

I ended the call and poked my head out of the giant dinosaur's tail.

"Looks like everybody's gone. . . ."

Gloria came out after me. Aidan followed her.

"So what's your name, man?" Aidan asked me.

"P.T."

"Solid. Easy to spell. Yo, I'm Aidan Tyler. The Tyes."

"Yeah," said Gloria. "We got that. I'm Gloria Ortega."

"Nice. You a fan?"

"Yes. Of Barbara Corcoran. She's an entrepreneur on *Shark Tank*. You ever watch that show?"

"Girl, I *own* a shark tank. Got me some piranhas in there, too."

"So who's this handsome young fellow?" asked Grandpa, who'd ambled over from his workshop to join us behind Dino. He was clicking his tongue like crazy. I could tell: he had a wad of white bread mustard-glued to the roof of his mouth. Again.

"Grandpa," I said, "this is Aidan Tyler. He's a mega-major superstar."

"Pleased to meet you, young man. I'm Walt Wilkie. And this, my friend, is your lucky day. Behold the Wonderland, the most wondrous motel under the sun!"

Grandpa spread his arms wide open to take in the glory of our motel. Then he smiled. I think he expected an orchestra to swell or fireworks to fill the sky. Something like that.

"Cool," said Aidan. "Nice meeting you, Pops. But I already have a crib."

"Oh, you have a baby in your room?"

"'Crib' is another word for 'place to stay,'" I explained to Grandpa. "Like I told you, Mr. Tyler is in town scouting locations for a new movie."

"It's an off-the-hook remake of those old beach party movies from the 1960s," said Aidan.

"Oh," said Grandpa. "I remember those. And I

remember all the dance moves, too. The Watusi. The Frug. The Shimmy. And, of course, the Swim."

He pinched his nose with one hand, raised the other hand high over his head, and wiggled down like he was diving underwater.

"That's cool, Pops. But this is, like, a total reboot. *Beach Party Surf Monkey*! Starring me, an Academy Award–winning actress, and a monkey."

"There's a monkey in the movie?" said Grandpa, sounding impressed. "Monkeys are good. Funny. Oh, the shtick a monkey can do . . ."

"Yo, this ain't no ordinary monkey, Pops," said Aidan. "This is YouTube sensation Kevin the Monkey!"

Now *I* was impressed.

"Mr. Tyler," I said, "we'd love to have you and Kevin film here. As you can see, the Wonderland is a one-of-a-kind location filled with—"

Aidan's phone thrummed in his board shorts.

"Yo. Gotta book. That's my ride."

He dug out a crinkled business card and handed it to me.

"Call my people. ASAP, dawg. Tomorrow's the big pitch day. Ciao for now."

He strutted out to Gulf Boulevard, where a stretch limo idled at the curb. We followed him.

"So where are you staying?" asked Grandpa.

"Next door. Conch Reef Resort. It's got that new-carpet smell. Plus, they're giving me frequent-stayer points. They also have a world-class buffet with deep-fried cheesy shark bites. I love me some cheesy shark bites. This is the Tyes. I'm out!"

He did a flashy back-and-forth arm thing with the "out."

A burly security guard in a dark suit and sunglasses opened the back door of the limo, and Aidan disappeared into the long black car so he could ride half a block up the street to the Conch Reef Resort.

The guys who wanted to buy the Wonderland so they could knock it down and bury us in the sand.

Remember the *Bounty*!

"So what was all that commotion out front?" asked Mom.

She'd been in her office crunching some more numbers when fate dropped Aidan Tyler into our laps.

"Our next big thing," I told her. "We won't ever have to sell out to Mr. Conch."

"Selling could be a smart move," said Mom. "We wouldn't have to worry about plumbing, or making beds, or fixing that pothole in the parking lot."

"I'm working on it," grumbled Grandpa, who, theoretically, was in charge of motel maintenance.

"But this could be huge, Ms. Wilkie!" said Gloria. "I see sock monkeys. Chocolate-dipped bananas."

"I see an inflatable King Kong," said Grandpa.

"Like they have at the used-car lot over on Thirty-Fourth Street North."

"Hold on," said Gloria. "We go to the barber shop, sweep up all their blond hair clippings, bag 'em, and sell 'em as Aidan Tyler's comb droppings!"

Mom just sort of stared at us.

"Um, first—ew. Second—who's this Aidan Tyler, and why would anybody want his comb droppings?"

I grabbed an old copy of *People* magazine I saw on the coffee table in the lobby. The cover was wrinkled and warped because someone had, I guess, used it as a coaster. But that didn't matter. Aidan Tyler was on the front.

"This guy," I told Mom. "He's *huge*. The new Justin Bieber. He's going to star in *Beach Party Surf Monkey* right here in St. Petersburg."

"They're scouting locations," added Gloria.

"They need a motel!" said Grandpa. "They're doing a remake of those old 1960s beach blanket movies that had Frankie Avalon and Annette Funicello. So what they need is an old-fashioned motel. Bingo! That's us! We're as old-fashioned as you can get!"

"They want to film here?" said Mom. "At the Wonderland?"

"Well," said Gloria, "it's not definite, but we have a shot."

"We have to pitch the producers tomorrow," I said. "There's going to be a lot of competition, but if we win, the Wonderland will be famous!"

"I don't know, you guys," said Mom. "I've heard horror stories about what happens when movie crews take over a location."

"Really?" said Grandpa. "From who?"

"My college friend Lindsey. She lives near Nashville and rented out her house for three days for a commercial shoot. They tore up her lawn, scratched the furniture, tied up traffic, annoyed the neighbors. . . ."

"We don't have a lawn," I said. "Just sand, pebbles, crushed seashells, and more sand. Plus, our neighbors, the Conches, are already annoying."

"According to my preliminary online research," said Gloria, tapping her phone, "you could gross between five and ten thousand dollars a day in location fees."

"And we could rent out all our rooms to the movie stars," said Grandpa. "The crew, too."

"If we did that," said Mom, who I think has a college degree in Being Practical, "we'd have to ask some of our regular guests to check out. Some of these folks have been coming here the same week for years."

"But, Mom," I pleaded, "we'll be famous!"

"Remember the *Bounty*?" said Grandpa, sort of randomly.

"That sailing ship that used to dock down by the pier?" said Mom.

Grandpa nodded. "It was the same boat they used in the movie *Mutiny on the Bounty,* starring Marlon Brando, back in 1962. For years, it was one of St. Pete's top tourist attractions. I took you there all the time when you were a kid, remember?"

Mom smiled.

"Sure," Grandpa continued, "it was just a wooden ship with a bunch of tall masts and a couple of cannons, but people paid money to stroll the decks because it made them feel like they were in the movies. We do this *Beach Party Surf Monkey* movie, the same thing will happen here!"

Mom shook her head. "If we really want to secure our future, I think we should seriously consider Mr. Conch's offer."

"Sell out?" gasped Grandpa. "Let him plow us six feet under so he can put in a new wing, another pool, and a fancy-schmancy spa with cucumbers and mud?"

"We could retire, Dad," said Mom, "and have enough to send P.T. to college."

"What is this? *Mutiny at the Wonderland*?"

Mom handed him a stack of papers. "Just look at the numbers. Numbers don't lie."

"Maybe not," said Grandpa. "But numbers don't make my heart sing, either. The Wonderland? She's just like that big sailing ship in the bay. She makes me smile whenever I see her!"

"But," said Mom, "if we don't sell out to Mr. Conch, our ship may sink!"

What Would Vince Lombardi Do?

"I still say we go for it," I told Gloria later when we were up in her room.

"Really?" said Gloria. "After all that pushback?"

"The Coco Palms, where Elvis Presley filmed the 1961 movie *Blue Hawaii,* stayed in business for decades afterward," I told her, because I'd just Googled it. "It was a hot tourist spot until a hurricane shut it down in 1992. It thrived for thirty years after it became a movie star! That could be us."

"Really?" said Gloria. "Is there a hurricane coming?"

"Kids," said Mr. Ortega, who was getting ready to head off to WTSP to do the weekend sports report, "always remember what the great Green Bay Packers coach Vince Lombardi once said: 'It's not whether you get knocked down; it's whether you get back up!'"

Taking that as parental permission to pursue our goal (even though, to be fair, Mr. Ortega had no idea what goal Gloria and I were pursuing), we pressed on.

After Mr. Ortega left for work, I put my phone in speaker mode and called the number on the business card Aidan Tyler had given us. We discovered that "Surf Monkey Productions" had set up shop at the Grand Hyatt hotel over in Tampa.

We also confirmed what Aidan Tyler had told us: they'd be listening to pitches from beachfront hotels and motels the very next day.

"From noon to three," said the guy who answered the phone. "But I gotta be honest with you, kids—we're all booked up. Sorry Aidan led you on like that. Right now we're leaning toward the Conch Reef Resort or the Don CeSar Hotel. They near you?"

I took a deep breath.

Mr. Conch was our competition?

"Yes, sir," I finally said. "The Conch Reef is right next door."

"Swell. Drop by someday during the shoot. We'll make sure you get a chance to meet the monkey."

And he hung up on me.

"That's it," said Gloria. "We don't stand a chance. They're booked up. And Aidan Tyler is already staying at the Conch Reef, the Don CeSar is already famous . . ."

"What about what your dad said?"

"Come on, P.T. Not even Vince Lombardi won every single game."

"Maybe not. But he definitely lost all the ones he quit before they were over."

"It *is* over. My guess? They'll pick the Don CeSar. It's retro-looking and it's a known known."

"Huh?"

She showed me her computer screen as she read her most recent search results.

"Hollywood's filmed a bunch of movies at the Pink Palace on St. Pete Beach. Including Ron Howard's 1985 Oscar-winning *Cocoon*!"

"I don't care," I told her. "We're going to the Hyatt in Tampa. Tomorrow. Between noon and three."

"Really? And how are we going to get to Tampa? Walk? Ask your mom to give us a lift? Hitch a ride with Mr. Conch?"

I smiled. "Nope. We'll ask Grandpa!"

∘ ∘ ∘

"The Grand Hyatt over in Tampa?" said Grandpa when we went to see him in his workshop. "I have a fishing buddy over there, John Adamo. Great guy. He practically runs the place. Don't worry—if anybody can get us into that meeting, it's Johnny Adamo!"

"Excellent!" I said.

"I'll start working up the charts for our Power-Point presentation," said Gloria.

"Charts?" Grandpa and I said at the same time.

"It's a meeting, you guys. You can't have a meeting without charts!"

"Oh," said Grandpa. "I did not know that. Thank you, Gloria."

"You're welcome, sir."

And then we raced back to her room to perfect our sales pitch.

Pitch Perfect?

The hallways outside the meeting rooms at the Grand Hyatt hotel in Tampa were packed with people in suits and ties from big-league hotel operations, all of them waiting to make their pitches to the movie producers inside the Snowy Egret conference room.

I did not see Mr. Conch, but I could smell his cologne. It lingers.

"I feel sorry for all those other guys," I said. "They don't have a chance, because they don't have your charts!"

Gloria grinned. "Thank you, P.T."

"Johnny said he'd meet us out back near the dumpster," said Grandpa.

"Shouldn't we try to go through the front door first?" asked Gloria.

"Why bother?" said Grandpa. "They're all booked up. The big boys got on the list before we could. Johnny is our best and only shot."

"If you don't mind me asking," said Gloria, "what exactly does your friend Mr. Adamo do here at the hotel?"

"He's a custodial engineer."

"A janitor?" I said.

"That's right."

"I thought you said he was in charge of the whole place."

"He is, P.T. Janitors always are."

We slipped out the back door and met Mr. Adamo near the loading dock, where he was heaving big black garbage bags into the dumpster. They made squishy, sloshing noises when they landed. They also stank. I think the bags were stuffed with the leftovers from the past week's crab fest.

"Johnny," said Grandpa, "this is my grandson, P.T., and his good friend Gloria Ortega."

"Pleased to meet you," said Mr. Adamo, extending his hand. Gloria and I both shook it. Afterward, our hands smelled like crab claws.

"You two are the kids who found the Miami hotel jewels over at that zoo!"

I smiled. It felt good to be famous.

"It was actually more of an animal sanctuary," I told him, "but, yeah, that was us."

"Well, come on," said Mr. Adamo, jingling the ginormous ring of keys dangling off his belt. "Let's get you into that conference room. You two are going to be the hotel's youngest room service runners." He checked his watch. "Because according to the master schedule, the Hollywood folks will be taking a refreshment break in five minutes. I borrowed a couple of uniforms from the laundry room so you guys can wheel in the cart."

"Awesome," I said.

Fact: janitors really are the best. At school or a hotel, there's no door they can't open.

Gloria and I slipped into a pair of white coats that had very long sleeves because we were a little shorter than most of the Hyatt's staff. Mr. Adamo hooked us up with a cart loaded down with chips, nuts, cookies, and a punch bowl filled with soft drinks bobbing around in a watery sea of ice cubes.

There was also one banana.

I wondered if it was for Kevin the Monkey!

Gloria placed her laptop on the cart's lower shelf, hiding it behind a tablecloth curtain.

"Good luck in there, you two," whispered Grandpa, giving us each a final pat on the back as Mr. Adamo unlocked the service entrance into the meeting room.

We rolled in.

There was a long table with a bunch of assorted

adults and one mysterious young girl hiding behind sunglasses. Kevin the Monkey wasn't there.

"I'm still liking the Don CeSar," said a guy wearing a baseball cap. He might've been the movie's director. Directors always wear baseball caps. I'm not exactly sure why. Baseball Cap got up, came over to our cart, and grabbed the banana.

"I'm with you, Kurt," said a lady in a very swanky business suit. "If the Don CeSar hotel was good enough for Ron Howard, it's good enough for me."

I pegged her as one of the producers. The other grown-ups were sitting behind place cards that spelled out their job titles: director of photography, designer, locations manager, choreographer.

The mysterious girl in the sunglasses?

She didn't have a sign telling us who she was.

And while all the grown-ups strolled over to help themselves to soda and snacks and talk about lighting this and shooting that and keeping Aidan Tyler out of trouble, the girl in the sunglasses didn't say a word.

She just sank deeper and deeper into her seat.

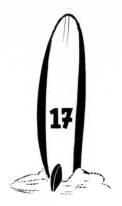

. . . And Action!

While the movie people gabbed and guzzled and grabbed snacks, Gloria snuck over to a round table in front of a screen so she could hook up her laptop to the LCD projector.

She gave me a nod and a wink.

We were ready to roll.

I shot her a thumbs-up. She hit the play button on the computer.

Pictures of the Wonderland filled the screen.

Music swelled. The soundtrack from *Star Wars*!

"Ladies and gentlemen," I said, "please excuse the interruption. But when you hear what we have to say, you'll be glad you shared your snack break with me, P.T. Wilkie; Gloria Ortega; and the wonderful Wonderland Motel on St. Pete Beach."

"Who the heck are you?" asked the guy in the baseball cap.

"The guy you need, Kurt," I told him. "Can I call you Kurt, Kurt?"

"No. You cannot."

"Okay. Don't really need to."

The girl in the sunglasses coughed out a little laugh when I said that.

"All I really need to do, sir, is show you these incredible pictures of the ideal location for *Beach*

I personally guarantee that Kevin the Monkey

Party Surf Monkey." I pointed at the screen. "You want retro and that whole sixties vibe? We've got it." I turned to the choreographer. "We even have an on-site dance expert for all your Frug, Watusi, and Shimmy needs." I did a few of Grandpa's groovy moves. The girl in the sunglasses laughed again.

Next I focused on the locations manager. "You want white, sandy beaches? We've got the whitest and the sandiest! In fact, our whole entire beach is

will go bananas for the Wonderland!

made out of one hundred percent USDA-approved sand in varying shades of white!"

That line made the girl crack up.

Next Gloria hit them with her charts.

"Ladies and gentlemen," she said, "P.T. and I represent the sweet spot of your target demographic. In short, we *are* your audience. In a recent random survey—"

"We called up some friends last night," I added.

The girl in the sunglasses was grinning like crazy.

Gloria continued. "Our respondents unanimously told us—and I quote—they would be 'stoked' to see a motel as 'totally awesome' as the Wonderland featured in a major motion picture."

"It *is* pretty funky," said the locations manager, rubbing his chin. "Retro chic."

"It's super funky," I said. "Because you can't fake this kind of kitsch."

("Kitsch" is a word Grandpa sometimes uses to describe all our wacky decorations.)

"And kids our age," I said, "the kids you want to buy tickets to your movie? Well, as your star, Aidan Tyler, might tell you, we like to 'keep it real, man.'"

"Authenticity coupled with an attractive location rental cost structure should streamline your decision-making process," said Gloria. "Hospitality is our core competency. The Wonderland is a quick win-win for *Beach Party Surf Monkey* and eager teen and tween moviegoers everywhere."

I started handing out brochures. "Don't take our word for it. Read these handy handouts."

"Are you kids done?" asked Kurt, the director.

"Yes, sir. We just didn't want you guys to make a colossal mistake and film in a parking garage like the Conch Reef Resort or show everybody the same old motel they've seen a billion times. Your movie isn't Ron Howard's *Cocoon* and this isn't 1985. In fact, it hasn't been 1985 for a long, long time, Kurt. I mean, sir. Or Sir Kurt."

When I said that, the mysterious girl in the sunglasses laughed so hard she nearly gagged on a mouthful of water. Gloria and I exchanged quick glances. We both knew we had this thing totally nailed!

"Thank you," said the producer lady. "It took real guts to bust in here and make your pitch. Very entertaining. We'll get back to you."

That's what she said.

But as we were leaving, I saw her slide our pamphlet off the edge of the table and into the trash.

Raining on Our Parade

On the drive home from Tampa, it started to rain.

Sometimes the weather knows exactly how lousy you're feeling and tries to make you feel even worse.

"You can't win them all," said Grandpa when he dropped us off outside the lobby. "But don't tell your father I said that, Gloria. I'm sure some football coach would disagree."

We dodged the raindrops and dashed into the lobby.

"Well," said Gloria, "since we won't be making a movie anytime soon, what do you want to do?"

"I don't know. What do you want to do?"

Gloria shrugged. "Whatever."

"I guess we could give tours of Dino the Dinosaur's butt," I suggested. "Tell people Aidan Tyler hid in there once."

"It'd be better if we had pictures or something to prove it," said Gloria.

"Yeah . . ."

"You've given us a lot to think about, Mr. Conch," said Mom, coming into the lobby with a phone glued to her ear. "I'd like to discuss your very generous offer with my family and our, uh, financial advisor."

She was looking at Gloria when she said that.

"Thank you," said Mom, ending the call.

"What's up?" I asked.

"We need to find Grandpa," said Mom, sounding way too chipper. "Mr. Conch just made a formal offer to buy the Wonderland."

"No," I said. "You can't let him demolish Grandpa's dream."

"It's a very tempting offer, hon. Mr. Conch has extremely deep pockets."

"Because he's hiding all sorts of sleazy deals inside 'em." Grandpa, soaking wet, came into the lobby. "I couldn't remember where I put my umbrella. Thought I might've left it in here."

"Mom wants us to sell out to Mr. Conch," I said.

"I didn't say that, P.T. I just told Mr. Conch we would give his offer serious consideration."

"Again with the seriousness?" said Grandpa. "What happened to *fun* in the sun? Since when did our state motto become 'Bored Out of Your Gourd'?"

"I think Ms. Wilkie is wise to consider all

long-term financial opportunities," said Gloria. "As unsettling and unattractive as they may be."

"Thank you, Gloria," said Mom. "I think."

The phone chirped. Mom picked it up.

"Hello? . . . Yes, this is the Wonderland Motel. . . . Really? I didn't even know we were under consideration."

She shot Grandpa and me a major look.

"Hang on," she said. "I'm going to put you on speaker. I suspect you really want to talk to my son and my father. . . . Oh, really?"

Now Gloria got the look.

"Yes, she's here, too. Hang on, Mr. Carnes."

She tapped a button on the phone.

"Why don't you tell them what you just told me?"

"Sure. Hi, guys. This is Cole Carnes, locations manager for *Beach Party Surf Monkey*."

"Hi, sir," said Gloria. "Thanks for your support in the meeting earlier."

"Hey, I loved your motel—the look, the feel, the whole funky retro vibe. More important, our star loves it. She doesn't want to film anywhere else."

"'She'?" I said. "I thought Aidan Tyler was the star."

"Sorry," said Mr. Carnes. "Aidan is the male lead. The female lead is Academy Award–winning actress Cassie McGinty. You met her at the Hyatt."

"I don't remember. . . ."

"She was the girl in the sunglasses."

Of course, I thought. *She had a good laugh.*

"Cassie doesn't say much in front of people she doesn't know," Mr. Carnes continued. "But after you kids left the room, she spoke up like crazy. Even called Lisa Norby Rook out in LA."

"And who, if I may ask, is Ms. Norby Rook?" Gloria inquired.

"Studio head at Dreamscope Pictures. She's the one who green-lighted this project and signs all our checks. So, what do you say? Want to make a movie together?"

"Are you kidding?" said Grandpa. "We'd love to. This is my big chance to catch up to that other Walt, the one over in Orlando!"

I looked at Mom.

"It's up to you, P.T.," she told me. "I love the idea of moving to Arizona, maybe hiking in Saguaro National Park. But it's *your* future I'm worried about most."

Grandpa was so excited he was doing that wiggle-dive-dance thing again.

This was so cool. No way could Mr. Conch knock down the Wonderland after it starred in *Beach Party Surf Monkey.* Too many fans would be upset. We'd practically be a landmark, like that Hollywood sign in, you know, Hollywood.

"Mom, tell Mr. Conch thanks but no thanks."

"We don't have to tell him anything right now," said Mom. "He gave us three weeks to make up our minds."

"I don't need three seconds," I said. "Mr. Carnes? You've got a deal. Let's make some movie magic!"

Our Number One Fan

The movie people and Mom worked out all the financial details while Gloria and I hit my room to learn all we could about Cassie McGinty.

"We need to find the synergy here," said Gloria. "She's the reason this deal went through. Right now, she's the Wonderland's number one fan. That means we need to become *her* number one fans, too."

"Do I have to shriek and stuff like those kids chasing Aidan Tyler?"

"No, P.T. She's not into all that. She's a very serious young actress who, according to this article in the *Hollywood Reporter,* is 'looking to lighten up a little and have some fun doing a goofy family movie about cute boys, hot surfing, and a hysterically funny monkey.' She also likes the idea of working with 'Kevin and the heroes at the Sunshine State Primate Sanctuary to promote animal welfare awareness.'"

It was a "major departure" for Miss McGinty, who was only fifteen, according to the *New York Times.* She'd just won an Academy Award for her supporting role in *Grief, Sorrow, and Woe,* which didn't really sound like a major laugh riot to me.

Mom worked the phone like crazy and was able to find all our regular customers rooms in other motels and resorts. Gloria helped her put together an incentive package, which included one night free on their next visit and a souvenir T-shirt.

About a dozen of them headed next door to the Conch Reef Resort.

"The carpets smell brand-new!" exclaimed Helen Nelson, from Toronto. "I could get used to this!" She'd been staying in the same room at the Wonderland for the same four weeks every year for two decades.

"I wonder if she'll ever want to come back," Mom said with a sigh after Ms. Nelson packed up and headed next door. "Our carpets smell like mildew."

"Don't worry," I said. "She'll come back. When you're famous, everybody is your friend!"

"We're not famous, P.T."

"No, Mom, but we're gonna be!"

In the afternoon, the cast and crew started moving into our newly vacant rooms. Kurt, the director, was upstairs, overlooking the parking lot. Dawn, the producer, took three rooms—one to sleep in, two to turn into the production office.

Aidan Tyler was still bunking down next door at the Conch Reef Resort, but I didn't care much. We had the really big stars: Cassie McGinty, who'd be checking in that afternoon, and my fave, Kevin the Monkey!

"We need to get some *Beach Party Surf Monkey* promotional items into our sales pipeline, fast," suggested Gloria. "I see Hawaiian leis. Palm tree toothpicks. Surfboard necklaces and earrings. Pineapples wearing sunglasses . . ."

"All great ideas," I said. "But who will we sell them to?"

"Our usual target audience, of course: tourists."

"But we don't have any of those staying with us anymore," I reminded her. "They all checked out so the movie people could check in."

"True. But we still have the parking lot and the Gulf Boulevard frontage."

We went around to the front of the motel to see where we might be able to set up shop.

And that was when the biggest star of them all pulled up in a van wrapped with bright green graphics for the Sunshine State Primate Sanctuary.

Kevin the Monkey had arrived!

Seeing Superstars

Kevin was a capuchin monkey.

Those are very smart primates. In his YouTube videos, Kevin was always doing incredible stunts.

Or throwing stuff. In one video, he shot hoops with a tiny basketball—including a two-arm over-his-head backward shot that was nothing but net!

"How'd you get Kevin to do all those tricks?" I asked J.J., the trainer.

"The same way we'll get him to surf in the ocean and ride a tiny Jet Ski around the swimming pool," she told me. "By making it fun. Kevin *loves* playing. So it's my job to make his work on the movie more like a game."

"When did you buy Kevin?" I asked.

J.J. shook her head. "We didn't buy him. We rescued him from the zoo where he was born. They'd taken Kevin away from his mother and sisters when he was only four months old and were trying to sell him as a pet. But you know what, guys?"

"What?" said Gloria.

"Monkeys make terrible pets. The worst. Fortunately, the zookeeper in charge of interviewing buyers realized that a cage in somebody's house would be the worst kind of life for Kevin. So she brought him to us."

"Awesome!" I said.

"Kevin was lucky," added Gloria.

"Us too," said J.J. "He's such a ham. He's been a great ambassador for all the other primates back home at the sanctuary."

Kevin chirped.

"He's hungry. We'd better go find our room and grab a snack. See you guys later."

J.J. and Kevin headed into the lobby.

"Isn't he awesome?" said a girl with her hair tucked into a baseball cap. She'd just strolled down the sidewalk, sipping an iced coffee drink. "The monkey, I mean."

"He's a major YouTube star," I told her.

"And animal sanctuary ambassador," added Gloria.

"He's Kevin the Monkey," I said. "Come back tomorrow and maybe you can have your photo taken with him."

"Or his cardboard cutout," said Gloria.

"True," I said. "Kevin himself won't be able to pose for photos with his fans. He'll be too busy, starring in a major motion picture, which, by the way, is being shot right here, at the soon-to-be-world-famous Wonderland Motel!"

"I know," the girl said with a laugh, taking off her hat and shaking out her hair. "I'll be working with him. I'm Cassie McGinty. We met the other day. Well, not officially. I guess we're doing that right now." She held out her hand. "Hi. I'm officially Cassie McGinty."

Gloria and I both hyperventilated for a second. Gloria recovered first.

"Pleased to meet you," she said. "I'm Gloria Ortega."

"I'm, uh, you know, uh, P. T. Wilkie."

(I was sort of nervous.)

"P.T. like P. T. Barnum?" Cassie asked.

I nodded. "One of my grandfather's heroes."

"Neat."

"Miss McGinty," I said, "we can't thank you enough for choosing our motel. You won't be sorry!"

She smiled. "I know. It looks so cool."

"It is," said Gloria. "Very cool."

"But not as cool as you," I said. "We know all about you!"

"You starred in diaper commercials when you were a toddler," said Gloria.

"You played a car accident victim on that hospital show when you were six!" I added.

"Your big breakthrough performance was in that thriller when you were seven," said Gloria.

"And that cop movie you did when you were eight . . ."

"Then there was the Academy Award . . ."

"And then you did Broadway . . ."

Cassie grinned. "It was nice officially meeting you guys. I guess I'd better go find my room." She took a step toward the lobby. Then she stopped and turned around. "You know the truth, guys? When you're famous, nobody really knows you."

She headed into the motel.

I stood there, confused.

Cassie McGinty had it backward.

When you're famous, *everybody* knows you.

Monkeying Around at School

The next day at school the art teacher, Mrs. Loweecey, helped me mount a life-sized cutout of Kevin the Monkey on foam core board.

The librarian, Ms. Wozniak, let me borrow her laminator so I could coat the figure with plastic. I was carrying the Kevin cutout down the hall to my locker when Mr. Frumpkes stopped me.

"What's that under your arm, Mr. Wilkie?"

"A capuchin monkey. They're native to Central and South America. They're super smart. They rub millipedes on their fur during mosquito season, because smooshed millipede gunk makes an excellent insect repellent! You should try it sometime, sir."

"Get to class, Mr. Wilkie."

"I have study hall this period."

"Then go study something."

"I am." I raised my Kevin cutout. "Capuchin monkeys."

Mr. Frumpkes stomped away in a huff.

Fact: I love when that happens.

Of course, everybody at school wanted to hear about the movie and Aidan Tyler and Cassie McGinty and Kevin the Monkey.

So during lunch, I once again regaled the crowd with tales of wonder. That means I entertained and delighted them. Regaling is what we Wilkies do best.

"Kevin the Monkey is busy rehearsing for the big surfing scenes," I told my audience. "Of course, they may want me to give Kevin a few pointers and show him a few moves, since, not too long ago, I outran a shark on my boogie board."

"How'd you do that?" asked Pinky.

"I let him take a bite out of the back. You ever try to chew Styrofoam? Very dry. Not very tasty. That shark forgot all about me and hightailed it back to the Bahamas for something sweet to wash away the taste."

"You are so awesome, P.T.!" said Kate Mackenzie Williams.

"Speaking of awesome," I said, "the other day, Gloria and I got to hang with Aidan Tyler *and* Cassie McGinty."

"Whoa!" went the crowd.

"What were they like?" said Kate.

"Pretty chill," I said. "We just, you know, hung out and stuff."

"Ooooh!"

"Hey, if you guys want to get a little closer to all the action, stop by the Wonderland Motel, 7000 Gulf Boulevard, this coming Saturday. We'll have all sorts of souvenirs, snack food items, and, of course, interactive movie activities."

"Woo-hoo!"

From the reaction in the cafeteria, I suspected the movie stuff would be the Wonderland's biggest hit ever.

After lunch Gloria asked me, "What sort of inter-active movie activities were you talking about?"

"I don't really know," I told her. "But we have all week. We'll think of something."

So after school, we brainstormed a ton of ideas.

We'd definitely be offering pictures of the stars. Those were super easy to find on the Internet. Gloria had some great banana-related ideas for the concession stand.

"And sock monkeys," she added. "Home-run idea? We make them out of Aidan Tyler's dirty socks. No. Wait. Scratch that idea. It's too gross."

"How about those Barrel of Monkeys toys that hook together in a string?" I suggested.

"Perfect!"

There were so many songs with "monkey" in the title. I wanted to change the lyrics to one so Pinky Nelligan could sing it in the parking lot—especially since his last parking lot gig ended early, thanks to Mr. Frumpkes.

My favorite tune? The theme from an old 1960s TV show starring a rock group called, believe it or not, the Monkees.

"We should sell their old albums, too!" said Gloria. She found a bunch on eBay for like a nickel each.

My biggest idea hit when I saw Grandpa puttering around the parking lot in his John Deere Gator cart. He was hauling the train cars from his recently restored ride-along railroad.

Watch out, Universal Studios Florida in Orlando, I thought. *You are in for some major St. Pete Beach competition!*

Back Lot in the Parking Lot

During the week, the film crew built sets and pulled together costumes.

They set up an RV camp in the front parking lot. They brought in their own generator and strung electric cables all over the place.

The music director booked a bunch of recording sessions at a Tampa studio for Cassie, Aidan, and the other singers in the cast so they'd have something to lip-synch to when the cameras started rolling.

Veronica Conch dropped by to admire all the activity.

Not really. She came over to gripe.

"These people should be at our hotel," she sneered at me. "It's way better than this dump."

I smiled and shrugged. "You win some, you lose some. But if they ever do a movie musical about a parking garage, I'm sure the Conch Reef Resort will be everybody's first-choice location."

Princess Veronica stomped away. When she did, a couple of sequins popped off her sneakers.

● ● ●

Before we knew it, it was Saturday morning.

Gloria, Pinky, and I were ready at seven a.m. Mom and Mr. Ortega came out of the lobby to lend us a hand.

Grandpa was sleeping in, but he'd drive the first "tram" around the "back lot" at nine a.m. I'd be the tour guide. Hey, I've been on the Jungle Cruise at Disney World a few times. I know how to spin a spiel.

"Well, this is it," said Mr. Ortega as Gloria set up a camp stove to melt Hershey's bars and make chocolate-dipped bananas. "Game day. You control your own destiny out here in the parking lot. Will you savor the thrill of victory or taste the agony of defeat?"

"Dad?" said Gloria.

"Yeah?"

"You really need a new phrase book. You use that 'agony of defeat' line all the time."

"Because it's a classic, Gloria. A classic!"

"Have fun today, hon," said Mom as I tidied up my stack of Maps of the Stars' Rooms (regular price $4.99, just $1.99 with every $10 tram ticket).

"Thanks," I told her. "Gloria thinks these tours will open up what she called a 'fresh revenue stream' for us."

Mom laughed. "We're doing fine, hon. You were right. With the location fees from the movie company and the premium room rates for their cast and crew, we might just have our best month ever!"

And then she kissed me. Just on the forehead, so we were still cool.

The movie crew was all set to start shooting first thing Monday morning. Kurt, the director, and Josh David, the set designer, were fine with us giving weekend tram tours.

A crowd of early birds started gathering in the parking lot around eight-thirty—mostly parents with their kids.

Including one of our neighbors who came with her son.

That's right.

Mrs. Frumpkes, who lives down the street, brought Mr. Frumpkes.

Our First Tour

"**M**y mother would like to see the monkey," said Mr. Frumpkes, bitterly biting out the words.

His lips were twitching as he faked a smile. Apparently, his mom *really* loved Kevin the Monkey.

"He's a hoot on the YouTube," she said. "That one where he snaps his fingers and plays the piano? Reminds me of Frank Sinatra. A-ring-a-ding-ding!"

"Well, Mrs. Frumpkes, Kevin is very busy rehearsing, but I have, occasionally, seen him lounging around the pool this early in the morning. So maybe we'll get lucky. But remember, no paw-tographs!"

Mr. Frumpkes handed me twenty dollars. I gave him back ten.

"Teacher discount," I said with a wink.

"Don't forget your T-shirts, sock monkeys, and frozen bananas, ladies and gentlemen!" hollered Gloria from her concession stand, where she was grabbing fistfuls of cash and stuffing them into a metal box. "The more you smell like bananas, the better the chance that Kevin the Monkey will come out to greet your group."

Mrs. Frumpkes made her son buy her a chocolate-dipped banana on a stick.

"Load 'em up, P.T.!" Grandpa said, then tooted his wooden train whistle. "This train is about to leave the station!"

Kurt, the director, who was staying in a front room on the second floor, came out on the balcony with a mug of coffee to check out the scene down in the parking lot. He looked like he was smiling. He was also swaying back and forth, bopping along to Pinky's version of the *Monkees* theme song.

It was showtime!

"Ladies and gentlemen, please notice there are two lines for the tram, one on the right and the other on the left. If you'd like to keep your family together, please stay in the same line. However, if there is someone in your family you'd like to get rid of, just put them in the opposite line and you'll never see them again."

Everybody laughed. Mrs. Frumpkes was eye-balling her son, maybe wondering what line to put him in.

As people climbed aboard, I kept up my patter. "By the way, if you lost a roll of fifty twenty-dollar bills wrapped in a red rubber band over by the concession stand, please let me know. I've got great news. We found your red rubber band."

More laughter. Kurt, up on the balcony, actually guffawed, which is like a laugh, only bigger.

I climbed into the front car.

"Hiya, sir," I said to a man in the first row. "Where are you from?"

"Chattanooga."

"I'm sorry?"

He said it louder. *"Chattanooga!"*

"Oh, I heard you the first time, sir. I'm just sorry."

More laughs. Even from the Chattanooga guy.

"Now, Grandpa, if you're ready to—"

I stopped in midsentence (something I seldom do, by the way).

From where the tram was parked in our front lot, I had a clear view of that giant glowing screen next door at the Conch Reef Resort. The billboard was blaring a brand-new image with scrolling headlines. It was a fanzine photo of Aidan Tyler looking super cheesy. Under him, strobing letters spelled out:

● ● ● ● ● ● ● ● ● ● ● ● ● ● ● ●

**AIDAN TYLER SLEPT HERE LAST NIGHT.
THIS MORNING HE ORDERED WAFFLES.
HURRY!
HE MIGHT STILL BE EATING BREAKFAST!**

● ● ● ● ● ● ● ● ● ● ● ● ● ● ● ●

Everybody on the tram saw the sign, too.

"Aidan's still there?" squealed a girl.

Several others shrieked.

"We'll take your second tour!" said Mrs. Frumpkes, climbing out of her seat. "I love that Aidan Tyler! Such a sweet young boy!"

Our entire crowd of early birds flew next door to take the Conch Reef Resort's Aidan Tyler Waffle Tour.

The Waffle Louse

"You guys guard the fort," I told Gloria and Pinky. "I'll head next door, find out what's going on."

"It's called competition, P.T.," said Gloria. "It is the backbone of the American free-enterprise system."

"No way," said Pinky. "Stealing customers? That's totally un-American."

"Competition brings out the best in products," said Gloria.

"And the worst in people!" I added. "Hang here. I'll be right back."

I hurried down the sidewalk with what had been *our* crowd. Aidan Tyler's illuminated face was still smirking smugly on the ginormous sign.

"Hey there, Petey."

Mr. Conch was holding open the front door to his world-class restaurant, ushering in the mob.

"Here to take the booth tour? It was Veronica's idea. She saw how popular all your gimmicks and stunts were next door, decided to outclass you. The kid's a chip off the old block. A high-quality daughter. I'm very, very proud of her, as I'm sure your dad is very, very proud of you."

I wasn't sure if Mr. Conch knew the real story about my father or was just saying the standard stuff grown-ups always say. Either way, I didn't rise to the bait.

"How much are you guys charging for your tour?" I asked.

"Nothing. It's free with every purchase of our best-in-the-world breakfast buffet, which includes Aidan Tyler's favorites: eggs, breakfast meats, and griddle items, plus a small orange juice—all for just fourteen ninety-nine. Because at Conch High-Quality Resorts, you always get what you want because I always get what I want—like bulk discounts from the bacon and pancake batter boys!"

"Riiiight."

"Maple syrup costs extra, of course."

"Of course."

"You would've played it the same way?"

"Yes, sir."

"Good to know, because you're a pro, Petey. A pro. En-joy. And when your mom sells out to me, don't worry—there will always be a job for a huckster like you at Conch Enterprises! You remind me of me. And that's a *huge* compliment, kid. Huge."

"Mom's not selling—"

Mr. Conch held up a hand. "We'll see. She still has time to mull it over. Is she mulling?"

I had to nod. "Yes, sir."

"Good for her. You see? At the end of the day, I always get what I want."

He gave me his shark smirk again.

"Excuse me, sir."

I squeezed into the crowded dining room.

Veronica Conch was near an empty booth,

giving *her* spiel to *her* first tour group. She was so giddy she was clicking her sparkly red tennis shoes together like Dorothy trying to go home in *The Wizard of Oz*.

"That's where Aidan Tyler sat, like fifteen seconds ago," she said. "And that's where he spilled his orange juice, which is kind of against the law in Florida. And see that fork stabbing that half-chewed chunk of waffle? He left that waffle chunk there. The wadded-up napkin, too."

"Is Aidan Tyler still here?" asked a tourist.

"No. He said he had to go 'chillax.' But you guys are super lucky. I'm a singer, just like Aidan. So I will now sing one of Mr. Tyler's biggest hits."

Honey, honey, honey, oooh,
Like honey, honey, honey, nooo,
Like honey, honey, honey, oooh,
I totally appreciate you!

If she sings another verse, she's going to start shattering the juice glasses.

"Excuse me," said a girl behind me when Veronica was (finally) finished. "Do you know anything about the movie tours next door?"

The entire restaurant gasped.

Because the girl asking the question was none other than Academy Award–winning actress Cassie McGinty. And this time, she was dressed like a glamorous movie star.

"I want to make sure I'm on the next tram ride!" she said, smiling at me.

"We'll be leaving in five minutes, Miss McGinty," I told her.

"Awesome! Then I've got to run. I want to be first in line!"

She bolted for the exit.

So did everybody else, except, of course, Mr. Conch and his daughter. They were both scowling at me.

I shrugged and grinned.

"Competition," I told them. "I hear it's the backbone of the American free-enterprise system."

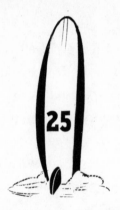

Back to the Back-Lot Tour

Cassie McGinty signed autographs and posed for photographs for like half an hour.

That meant Gloria sold a ton of frozen bananas. She even broke out our leftover candy jewelry, which, instead of being souvenirs commemorating the Sneemer brothers' stay at the Wonderland, was "repackaged and repurposed" as "Edible Hollywood Glamour Gear."

It totally helped that while signing and posing, Cassie wore a jawbreaker bracelet and a pair of gummy bear earrings.

When everybody in the crowd was happy, Cassie's cell phone rang.

"Excuse me, guys," she said. "I need to take this."

I looked up to the second-floor balcony.

Kurt, the director, was up there on his phone.

"Really?" said Cassie. "Total rewrites? Yes, sir. Well, I wanted to take the tram tour but . . . Yes, sir. You're right, sir. Work comes first."

Cassie hung up. Kurt hung up.

Then he shot me a wink.

Yes, I think the two of them were in cahoots.

"I'm sorry, everybody," Cassie told the crowd. "But that was my director."

"Ooooh!" The crowd was impressed. "Her director!"

"Apparently, the screenwriter has made some major rewrites for the scenes we're shooting first thing Monday morning. That means I have to go to work memorizing my new script. I can't take the tram ride."

"You're a real pro, Miss McGinty," said Mrs. Frumpkes. "We need more gals like you. You go do your homework—just like my son's students should do, even though they don't, because Francis is what the kids these days call a wimp."

"Mother?" whispered Mr. Frumpkes.

Cassie kept smiling at her adoring fans. "It was great meeting all of you! Have fun on the tour. Maybe you'll meet Kevin!"

She waved. The crowd cheered. And Cassie scampered off to her room to study her script or maybe watch a good movie on HBO. It's free at the Wonderland.

The Quest for Kevin

I reloaded the train cars.

Grandpa tooted his whistle and drove us around a block of rooms as we headed toward the pool, which is behind our main building.

"Where is Kevin the Monkey?" squawked Mrs. Frumpkes, her mouth full of melting mashed banana. "That Cassie McGinty is sweet, but I really came here to see Kevin."

"He might be around back," I said. "So make sure your eyes are like a banana. Keep 'em peeled! Now, as we approach the pool, you will notice the groovy 1960s cabana, complete with spinning mirror ball. This is where we'll shoot the first big scene on Monday!"

"*Ooooh!*" Up went the cell phones as everybody snapped a picture of the tent and shiny silver ball.

"There's Kevin!" shrieked Mrs. Frumpkes, frantically waving what was left of her chocolate-dipped banana toward our Muffler Man statue. Grandpa had come through. By painting on a mask, giving the giant a striped shirt, and strapping an inflatable Garfield pool toy in his hands, Grandpa had turned our Muffler Man into a cat burglar.

While J.J. looked on, Kevin scampered up one of the big guy's legs like it was a tree in the rain forest. He climbed out on the arms and jumped into the wobbly pool float.

Every single camera started clicking away. Kids were laughing.

They went absolutely nuts when Kevin used the inflatable cat as a big orange trampoline. I started cracking everybody up with corny monkey jokes I'd memorized from a website.

Folks, what do you call a monkey at the North Pole? Very lost.

"Don't worry about Kevin, ladies and gentlemen. When he needs to get down, I'm sure he'll just slide down the banana-ster. Of course, like most monkeys, Kevin doesn't like to play cards in the jungle. Too many cheetahs out there."

Mrs. Frumpkes cracked up.

Mr. Frumpkes did not. He looked miserable.

Our first backstage tour was definitely a much bigger hit than Veronica Conch's waffle booth bit. We did six more tours and were sold out of frozen bananas and candy jewelry by noon.

Then the day got even better.

Cassie McGinty asked Gloria and me if we wanted to eat lunch with her!

The Lunch Bunch

Cassie, Gloria, and I met up in the poolside cabana.

That way, Cassie could hide behind one of the tent flaps, where nobody could see her. She was back in her non-movie-star clothes—khaki shorts, flip-flops, and a T-shirt.

"So, do you like crabs and stuff?" I asked. "There's a pretty cool seafood shack across the street."

"I really can't go to restaurants," Cassie said with a sigh. "Not even McDonald's or Burger King."

"The price of fame?" asked Gloria.

"Exactly. What I'd really love is an old-fashioned bologna sandwich on white bread with lots of yellow mustard and maybe some pickle relish."

My jaw nearly dropped.

"You're kidding."

"Nope. It's so, I don't know, normal! A bologna sandwich and rippled potato chips. The generic grocery store kind. Those are always greasier than the name-brand chips."

Gloria and I both grinned.

"Well," I said, "have we got just the guy for you."

And that's how we all ended up in Grandpa's workshop, whipping up a platter of sandwiches, filling a bowl with Publix dip-style potato chips, and passing around a tube of Double Stuf Oreos.

Grandpa dug an icy can of Tahitian Treat fruit punch out of the cooler where he keeps his Cel-Ray and "other exotic and exquisite drinks." He offered it to Cassie.

"It's no Cel-Ray," said Grandpa with a shrug, "but it's still delicious. Very fruity. Very punchy."

"Remember when I was little, we had that statue of Punchy, the Hawaiian Punch kid, near the pool?" I said.

Grandpa grinned. "And I'd say, 'How about a nice Hawaiian Punch?' You'd say, 'Sure!' and I'd act like I walloped you in the stomach."

"Then I'd spin around and do a cannonball into the pool!"

"Best cannonball dive I ever saw," said Grandpa. "P.T. would splash out half the pool."

"A couple of weeks ago," added Gloria, "we organized an official cannonball contest here at the Wonderland."

"So are you guys like business partners?" asked Cassie.

"I guess," said Gloria. "Mostly we're just friends."

Cassie sighed the way Mom does when Mr. Ortega's in the room. "That must be nice."

"Nice?" I said. "It's awesome. And, by the way, I won that particular cannonball competition."

"He earned extra points for wearing the wildest bathing suit," said Gloria.

"Because I play to win!"

"If your movie needs a splashy cannonball diver," added Gloria, "P.T. is your guy."

"Great," said Cassie with a smile. "I'm going to remember that."

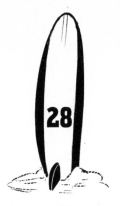

A Star Is Born?

After our lunch break, Gloria and I went back to work.

Well, actually, first she went back to Publix to buy more bananas and Hershey's bars.

Pinky Nelligan was strolling around again, strumming his guitar, crooning his *Monkees* song.

Meanwhile, Kurt, the director, came down from his second-story perch.

"Hey," he said. "I'm Kurt Stroh."

"I'm P. T. Wilkie, sir. That's short for Phineas Taylor."

"Just like P. T. Barnum, huh?"

"Yes, sir."

We shook hands.

"Sorry I wasn't more supportive when you kids pitched this motel over in Tampa," he said. "But you kind of took me by surprise. Plus, Aidan Tyler had been giving me all kinds of grief. . . ."

He swatted his hand at the air like he really didn't want to talk, or think, about Aidan Tyler, at least not on his day off. So I changed the subject.

"I admire all your work, sir," I said.

Gloria had insisted I learn everything I could about every single member of the cast and crew, especially the stars and the director.

"I particularly loved how you made that movie musical *Put On Your Shoes* so hip, even though it was about barefoot street urchins in Victorian England."

"We had a lot of fun with that one," said Kurt, proudly rolling back on his heels. "And please, call me Kurt."

"Yes, sir, Kurt."

"I heard your spiel earlier—when you were loading the tourists onto the tram."

"Oh, I hope I wasn't making too much noise."

"Not at all. It was hysterical. *You're* hysterical. How'd you like to be in my movie?"

"Really? Which movie are we talking about?"

He laughed. "See? You crack me up. We need a bunch of kids your age to fill out the background. You'd be in all the crowd scenes, so you'd have to miss a couple weeks of school. But don't worry. We'll have on-set tutors to make sure you keep up with your studies."

Missing school while being in a movie?

Hello?

Twist my arm.

"I'd love to do it," I said.

And then I took a gamble.

"And so would my two friends Gloria and Pinky."

"Is Pinky the guy on guitar?" Kurt asked.

"Yes, sir."

"Amazing Irish tenor voice. We'll put him in the chorus. What about Gloria?"

"She's extremely savvy when it comes to business."

"Tell you what—Gloria can be an extra with you.

Or if she's interested, we'll make her a production intern, have her work with Dawn Foxworth's folks in the business office."

"I'm sure she'd love that, sir . . . I mean, Kurt!"

And that's why the first day of the Wonderland Studio Tours was also the last.

The three of us were changing careers.

We were all going into the movie business!

Extra Breakfast

On Monday morning, I was in the "holding" area with a bunch of other "background" actors.

"They used to call us extras," explained one of the older kids. "But that made us sound so superfluous, you know what I mean?"

I nodded, even though I didn't.

I went over to what movie people call the craft services table.

I was expecting to find felt, scissors, and maybe some yarn. You know—crafts. Instead, I found all sorts of free snacks and drinks. Turns out if you're one of the "crafts" working on a movie, they have to feed you all day long. In the morning, the table was loaded down with bagels, doughnuts, breakfast burritos, cereal, cinnamon buns, oatmeal, sliced salmon, papaya. You name it. If it's ever been a breakfast food anywhere in the world, it was there under that tent.

Cassie came over to pour a cup of hot tea.

"This is fantastic," I said with my mouth full of food. "I mean, for me and my friends. I guess you must be used to it."

"No," she said with a smile. "It's still pretty fantastic."

"Miss McGinty?" said Gloria, coming over with a clipboard and looking extremely official with a walkie-talkie clipped to the belt of her cargo shorts. She'd opted for the production intern post. "They need you in makeup."

"Then I'd better go. Catch you guys later."

Cassie hurried off to one of the first-floor production rooms.

"You too, P.T.," said Gloria.

"Huh?" My mouth was still full of food. She caught me in mid-jelly-doughnut chomp.

"You need to go to makeup."

"Nah. In case you've never noticed, I don't wear makeup."

"P.T.? This is a movie. *Everybody* wears makeup. Otherwise, the lights will make you look all pale and pasty."

"Oh. Okay. Where do I go?"

Gloria checked her clipboard. "Stars are

doing makeup and hair in rooms 111 and 112. Extras—"

"You mean background actors."

"Right. You should report to the tent they set up over by the Muffler Man."

"Great."

"Catch you later. I need to check in with Aidan Tyler. Dawn wants me to 'shadow' him today."

She took off.

I headed to the makeup tent, where Pinky was hanging out with a bunch of the other singers in the chorus. All of a sudden, he snapped his fingers, and they launched into an amazing four-part-harmony a cappella pop song from that movie *Pitch Perfect*.

After the group hit (and held for, like, forever) their last high note, everybody sat down so the makeup people could smear our faces with something they called pancake.

When a wet spongeful of it hit my face, I understood why. It felt like the cold glop you get when you mix Bisquick with tap water.

After I was all made up and in my costume (Hawaiian shirt, baggy swimsuit, flip-flops), Mom and Mr. Ortega came over, excited about the first day of shooting.

"This is amazing, P.T.!" said Mom. "I never knew it took so many people to make a movie."

"Well," said Mr. Ortega, "in the words of the immortal Yogi Berra, 'you can observe a lot by just watching.'"

We all laughed.

Until we heard Aidan Tyler screaming.

At Gloria!

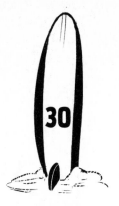

Meltdown

"I told you, girl—don't let those nasty blue M&M's melt all over the green ones!"

Aidan threw a fistful of candy to the ground near the ice machine. He was surrounded by his entourage—a group of flunkies who did stuff for him. One was in charge of his hair, another his face, a third his costume. The other six hangers-on just seemed to be there in case he needed anything else. All of them were scowling at Gloria.

She just stood there. Scowling back. Hard.

"You called me out of my trailer too soon, fool. That's why my M&M's are making a chocolaty mess and disrespecting me. That cuts deep, man."

"I called you when the director told me to call you," said Gloria, not backing down an inch.

"We should go over there," I said to Mom and Mr. Ortega. "Protect her."

Mr. Ortega held up his hand to stop me. "We'll blow the whistle and toss a penalty flag *if* we need to. But, P.T.? Gloria knows how to handle herself. Just watch."

"What's your problem, anyway?" Gloria snapped at Aidan. "Every single M&M tastes exactly the same, no matter what color!"

"Who do you think you're hating on, girl? I'm Aidan Tyler. The Tyes. You're just my gofer. When I want something, you go fer it."

"Actually," said Gloria, "my official title is production intern and—"

"Hey, Aidan," said Cassie, strolling over.

I could tell the Tyes just realized an Academy Award–winning actress had witnessed his entire M&M's meltdown.

"Oh, hey, Cee McG."

"Problem?"

"For real. This girl. She's, like, messing with my head space."

"Gloria?" said Cassie. "No way. She's the best production intern I've ever worked with. And I've worked on, oh, two dozen movies. This is what? Your first?"

"Yeah," mumbled Aidan.

I saw some of the crew members grin. Apparently, they were all familiar with our male star's temper tantrums. Two lighting guys working near me started swapping stories:

"I hear he locked his producer inside the men's room of a recording studio once," whispered one. "For three days."

"I hear he punched his fist straight through a birthday cake," whispered the other. "At Chuck E. Cheese's. And it wasn't his cake *or* his birthday."

"You want me to grab you some fresh M&M's?" Cassie asked Aidan. "I have some in my trailer."

"Nah," said Aidan. "I appreciate you, Cee McG, but no worries. I'm good."

"You guys ready to shoot this first scene or what?" asked Gloria.

"Yeah," said Aidan. "I guess."

"Cool," said Cassie. "Let's go."

Gloria led the two stars toward the swimming pool.

"See?" said Mr. Ortega. "Poor boy never had a chance."

Beach Party Surf Monkey

Okay—here's a quick synopsis of the script for *Beach Party Surf Monkey.*

It's a funny story about the most famous monkey in the surfing world helping his friend Polly Pureheart (played by Cassie McGinty) find true love.

While hanging out on St. Pete Beach during Spring Break 1966, Polly, who's a hippie, and all her hippie friends meet Eric Von Wipple (Aidan Tyler), who's a snooty preppy (he wears a blazer and bow tie with his lime-green shorts) from some rich-kid boarding school up north.

Preppies and hippies are like coconut oil suntan lotion and water. They don't mix well together.

Pinky and I are playing some of the kids hanging out at the Wonderland Motel when Polly, Surf

Monkey, and their hippie friends meet Eric Von Wipple and his prepster pals for the first time.

Pinky is singing with the hippie choir. I stand in the background, taking up space.

One other thing: when they make a movie, they don't shoot the story in order, so it's kind of random and confusing.

We were going to start with a big scene in which Aidan's preppy meets Cassie's hippie for the first time while everybody else sings and dances and Kevin the Monkey rides a Jet Ski around the swimming pool.

J.J., from the primate sanctuary, walked Kevin (who was wearing board shorts) to the pool and helped him onto his tiny Jet Ski, which looked sort of like a floating bumper car with handlebars.

One thing I learned before the first take?

When you're an actor in a movie, it's different from when you're in a home video.

You're never supposed to wave at the camera.

Take One!

"**Q**uiet on the set!" shouted the assistant director, a big, burly bear of a guy named Steve, who everybody called Dawg.

"Scene 701," said a lady holding a clapper board in front of the camera lens. "Take one."

"No waving, people!" Dawg hollered, and, yes, he was looking straight at me.

Kurt, the director, pointed at Aidan Tyler.

"Aaaaaand . . . action!"

Aidan and his group of preppies strutted up to the pool.

"Like, pardon me, man," mumbled Aidan.

"Cut!" cried Kurt. "Aidan? You can't mumble your lines. And there's no 'like' in the script."

"Sorry, man."

"No 'man,' either."

"For reals?"

"Yeah."

"Awesome. Let's try that again."

We did. Eleven more times.

Finally, forty minutes later, on take twelve, Aidan was able to say his whole first line.

He sounded stiff, the way I had in my third-grade Healthy Vegetables pageant, when I played the pumpkin.

Then he gestured at Kevin.

With an arm jab.

After he finished talking.

Behind the camera, the director was tugging at the hair on both sides of his head.

Fortunately, it was Cassie's turn to talk.

"That's no motor scooter," she said. "It's a boogie bike! And that's no gorilla. That's Surf Monkey!"

I was in the background, ten feet behind Cassie, but I could tell, by checking the angle of the camera lens, that I might be in the shot. Sort of. It was possible that people all over the world would see my elbow. It wasn't much, but it was my first step on the road to worldwide fame!

"Hey, dudes, surf's up!" cried Pinky, because, yes, they had actually given him a real line.

"Far out, man!" shouted all the hippies.

Humongous speakers blasted the playback of a

rocking Surf Monkey song while everybody launched into a big dance number.

Aidan Tyler? He just sort of stood there, bobbing his head from side to side.

The special effects team sent Kevin the Monkey flying around our swimming pool on his miniature Jet Ski. He rode it up a ramp and shot over our frog slide! It was awesome.

Go, Surf Monkey, you're ripping up the swimming pool!

What made it even cooler?

When they played back the first take on a big video monitor, I could totally see my elbow!

I was in the movie!

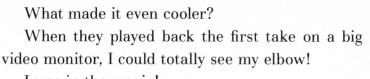

Go, Surf Monkey, you're running a surf boarding school! You are so cool, the girls all drool for Surf Monkey!

Take Thirteen

After take twelve, Cassie, Kurt, Aidan, and Dawg huddled around the playback monitor.

"We got that, bro!" said Aidan. He raised his right palm to slap somebody a high five.

Kurt and Cassie left him hanging. Dawg, too.

"It's missing something," I heard Kurt mutter. "We can cut around Aidan, smooth out his line reading in post. But . . ."

"But what?" snapped Aidan.

"It needs another bit of business," said Cassie. "A kicker. A final punch."

"How about I wink at the camera?" suggested Aidan. "Chicks dig it when I wink at 'em."

Aidan winked.

Everybody behind the camera just stared at him.

Finally, Cassie said, "It needs a button. One final joke. Something silly . . ."

Aidan raised both hands and backed up a step. "Aiyyo. My manager specifically said he didn't want me doin' nothing silly. Nobody wants to buy love songs from a clown, man."

Kurt leaned back in his director's chair.

I thought he was looking at me.

All of a sudden, Cassie started looking where Kurt was looking.

"P.T. would be perfect!" said Cassie.

Then she leaned in and whispered something in Kurt's ear.

"Love it! J.J.?" he called to the animal trainer, who joined the video monitor cluster with Kevin the Monkey riding on her shoulder. "Can Kevin do that jump over anything?"

"Sure. We just need to move the underwater ramp."

"Excellent," said Kurt. "Move it to the far end of the pool near the diving board. Dawg?"

"Yeah, boss?"

"We're going to upgrade a background player. The kid in the funny-looking swim trunks over there."

Hey, I might've been wearing my loudest bathing suit, but that doesn't mean it was funny-looking. It just had swirling purple paisleys that made me look like I had bruised amoebas swimming up my legs. It was the same suit I'd worn when I won that cannonball contest.

Which is what they wanted me to do now—because Cassie McGinty remembered the story we'd told her over lunch. Fact: sometimes all you need is a good story to take you from an elbow in the background to a featured actor in the scene.

The A.D., Dawg, came over, took me by my famous elbow, and guided me toward the diving board end of the pool.

"Think you can re-create your famous championship cannonball dive for us?" he asked.

"Sure. I guess."

"Great. We need you to do it right before Kevin the Monkey circles the pool and hits his jump ramp. You hop into the pool . . ."

"And he flies through my humongous splash?"

"Exactly. Everybody thinks it'll be funnier than the jump over the frog slide. It's stunt work. And you'll get wet. So you'll get paid extra. Do you have an agent?"

"Yes," said Gloria, stepping forward. "But I won't charge you the standard ten percent commission, P.T."

"Thanks."

"We'll work out the details after we wrap," said Dawg. "If that's okay with your agent."

"In this instance, yes," said Gloria.

"Cool. You ready to do this thing, P.T.?"

"Yeah!"

"Shout 'cowabunga' when you dive in," cried the director.

Wow. I had a scene *and* a line.

Well, a word, anyway.

This was definitely my big break! I was on my way to movie stardom.

story cont.
page 24

Change of Scenery

"**A**nd cut!" shouted the A.D. when they were finished shooting the scene.

I climbed out of the pool and everybody applauded!

(Well, everybody except Aidan Tyler. He was busy checking texts and tweets on his phone.)

"Way to go, P.T.," said Cassie.

"Hysterical, man," added Pinky.

"Let's reset!" cried the A.D. "Wardrobe? Dry P.T. down so he can go again!"

About six people attacked me with towels and whirring hair dryers.

"Um, are we going to do that whole thing again?" I asked.

The wardrobe gang laughed.

"Yes," said one of the guys blasting me with a hot-air gun. "About eight hundred times."

"Welcome to show biz, kid!" said a lady with a towel.

"Let's get him a fresh set of clothes," said Kurt through his bullhorn. "And, P.T.?"

"Yes, sir?"

"Do it exactly the same—only, this time, make it even funnier."

"Yes, sir!"

I hurried to one of the wardrobe RVs so I could change into a dry swimsuit and a fresh Hawaiian shirt. Gloria met me there. She was holding a stack of brightly colored swim trunks.

"I ran down the block to the Surf Shack," she

told me. "If one of their swimsuits ends up in the movie, both of us get free sunblock for a year."

"Huh?"

"It's called product placement, P.T. Hurry up. They're waiting for you on set."

I changed clothes in the RV.

When I came out in my new costume, Mr. Conch and a guy in a yellow construction helmet who looked like Bob the Builder's ugly brother were in the parking lot, gesturing at our spaceship.

"That hunk of junk's definitely gotta go," said Mr. Conch. "Get it outta here!"

"No problem, chief," said the construction guy.

"Oh, hi, Petey," said Mr. Conch, crinkling his nose at me. "Nice outfit. Those your swim trunks?"

"It's for the movie. What are you guys doing here?"

"Thinking. Planning. Brainstorming quality hospitality improvements. It's what I always do, kid. Twenty-four-seven."

"But we're not selling our property to you."

Mr. Conch laughed. "You hear that, Darryl? They're not selling."

The construction guy laughed.

"Kids," said Mr. Conch. "Am I right?"

"Fuhgeddaboudit," said Darryl.

"Seriously, sir," I said. "This movie will make the Wonderland so famous—"

"P.T.?" a voice boomed through a megaphone. It was Dawg, the A.D. "We needed you on set five minutes ago!"

"Have fun, Petey," said Mr. Conch as he and the construction guy ambled over to talk about burying the garden patch where Mom grows rosebushes.

"P.T.?" Dawg's voice boomed again.

I hustled back to my post on the diving board.

I had to focus on the movie. If it was a hit, Mr. Conch wouldn't be able to do any kind of hit job on our motel.

"You ready?" asked Gloria when I took my position at the edge of the pool. She could tell my brain was somewhere besides on location.

"Yeah."

I quickly thought about flailing my arms to make the dive funnier, but if I wasn't fully tucked when I hit the water, that might take away from my big splash. Plus, my arm flailing might distract Kevin the Monkey in the middle of his jump.

It's tough being a movie star. You have to think about so much stuff, but they don't give you a lot of time to think about it. Plus, I was still thinking about Mr. Conch taking a wrecking ball to Grandpa's rocket.

"Scene 701," said the lady with the clapper board, holding it in front of the camera lens again. "Take fourteen."

"Quiet on the set!" shouted the A.D.

"Aaaand . . ."

Before Kurt could say "action," I heard a very loud, very annoying noise.

And this time it wasn't coming from Aidan Tyler.

Quiet on the Set

"Hold the roll!" shouted the soundman, whipping off his headphones and killing the playback on the Surf Monkey song.

When he did, all anybody could hear was the rattling clink of a heavy chain coupled with the throaty rumble of a motor.

It was coming from next door.

The Conch Reef Resort.

Man, oh, man, I thought. *They are totally trying to sabotage us!*

Dawn Foxworth, the producer, who had been sitting in a director's chair behind the camera next to Kurt, marched over to the pool. Mr. Carnes, the locations manager, followed her.

"P.T.? Gloria? Ms. Wilkie?" said the producer.

We need to go next door and have a word with your neighbors. Kurt?"

"Yes, Dawn?"

"Take an early lunch."

"That's lunch," said Kurt.

"That's lunch!" boomed Dawg.

"Lunch!" shouted all the crew heads.

"We're eating next door at the Conch Reef Resort's buffet," announced Dawg. "Thirty minutes and then we're back in."

As you might recall, the Wonderland doesn't have a restaurant. The Conch Reef Resort, on the other hand, has those World-Famous Grouper Fingers with Tartar Sauce. So even though Mr. Conch was more or less our number one enemy at the moment, we were basically giving him a ton of money (I guess to make it easier for him to buy the Wonderland if the movie flopped).

The entire cast and crew trooped over to the world-famous buffet—except Aidan Tyler, Cassie McGinty, and Kevin the Monkey. They'd be eating in their air-conditioned trailers. Cassie was having a leafy-green smoothie. Kevin was munching monkey kibble. Aidan was probably popping more M&M's into his mouth. Just the green ones.

While everybody else grabbed lunch, Mom, Gloria, and I went searching for the source of the clinking and clanging with the movie's producer and locations manager.

It was pretty easy to find.

Veronica Conch was out back, near the Conch Reef Resort's kidney-shaped pool, watching a crane install—are you ready for this?—a thirty-foot-tall statue of a buccaneer.

"Isn't it sweet?" she shouted. "Daddy gave it to me!"

Wait a second! We do wacky statues, not Veronica Conch!

CLINK
CLANK
CLUNK

Yo-Ho-Ho?

"**H**ey there, Mrs.—I mean, *Ms.* Wilkie," said Veronica Conch as the fiberglass pirate creaked into place behind her. "Oh, hi, Ms. Foxworth, Mr. Carnes. My father and I met you guys over in Tampa when you were looking for a location but didn't pick ours. Remember? Is everything okay?"

"Is your father available?" asked Ms. Foxworth.

"Nuh-uh. He and the construction engineer just left to go talk to some lawyers because we need to knock down more shabby old motels that nobody wants to stay in anymore. Daddy's closing another mega-huge deal. Hey, speaking of deals, Ms. Wilkie, are you guys ready to sell your motel to Daddy because he always gets what he wants?"

"No," I answered. "We're too busy making a major motion picture!"

"I know. I heard the song about the monkey. Gosh, that sure was loud."

"Not as loud as your crane!"

"What's going on over here?" said Grandpa, joining us by the Conch Reef pool. When he saw the giant pirate statue, he nearly dropped his can of Cel-Ray.

He did belch.

"Is that one of mine?" said Grandpa. "Young lady, did you steal that pirate from us?"

Veronica scoffed. "Hardly. Do you think you guys are the only ones on Gulf Boulevard who can attract customers with goofy statuary? This is Pirate Pete and he's all ours!"

"Veronica," said Gloria, "I don't know if you realize this, but Surf Monkey Productions arranged for their entire cast and crew to take their lunch here at your restaurant today."

"Well, it *is* the biggest, best, and most bountiful buffet on the beach. Try saying that three times fast."

Gloria kept going. "That's one hundred and twenty-six lunches at fifteen dollars apiece, which equals one thousand eight hundred and ninety dollars in revenue for your restaurant. Comparing that with your average daily sales . . ."

"Wha-hut? How'd you get those numbers?"

"Immaterial. Eighteen hundred and ninety

dollars is triple your typical lunch take. Surf Monkey Productions had planned on buying one hundred and twenty-six more lunches tomorrow . . . if . . ."

"If what?" asked Veronica, blinking a lot.

"You can keep the noise down over here!" snapped Ms. Foxworth.

"Well, there's no need to get all snippy about it, ma'am. Golly, you Hollywood people sure are pushy."

"What Ms. Foxworth is trying to say," said Gloria, "is we'd sincerely appreciate your cooperation. In return, we won't be calling Crabby Bill's Casual Seafood Shack down the block to make alternate lunch arrangements."

"Oh. I see. This is what they call playing hardball."

"Correct."

Veronica nodded.

"Daddy does it all the time. So when, exactly, is your lunch break over?"

"Half an hour," said Ms. Foxworth.

"No problem. The crane guys should be finished by then."

"Wonderful."

"We just need to get it set up for our big promotional event this weekend. Will you be filming this weekend?"

"No."

"Good. Because we expect to attract quite a crowd. We're doing our first-ever Pirate Chest Treasure Quest. I'm printing up treasure maps, burying a chest filled with sparkly goodies. . . ."

I couldn't believe it.

Neither could Grandpa.

"That's our gig!" he said.

"You mean that *used* to be your gig," said Veronica with a big smirk.

Fact: while the Wonderland was busy making movies, Veronica Conch was swooping in and stealing our best ideas. Gloria and I had already done a Pirate Chest Treasure Quest!

"By the way," said Veronica, "would you and your movie crew like to eat *breakfast* in our restaurant, too? If so, I can double-triple guarantee there won't be any more noise problems."

Read all about it in Welcome to Wonderland: Home Sweet Motel. Available wherever fine books are sold.

I'm P. T. Wilkie and I approve this fake ad.

Gloria nodded with what looked like reluctant admiration. "You're good, Veronica—if not entirely ethical."

"Ethics don't put pennies in my piggy bank."

"I see. Is that your personal motto, Veronica?"

"No, it's Daddy's. So do we have a deal or what?"

"You have a deal," said Ms. Foxworth.

Veronica triumphantly pumped her arm. *"Ka-ching!"*

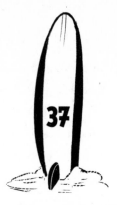

Back to the Background

By the end of the day, I'd done so many cannonballs into the pool I had to sit on a pillow to eat dinner.

And my toes were all sorts of wrinkly. They reminded me of a box of those weird golden raisins.

But such is the price of fame.

The next day, I was back in the makeup tent at six o'clock—in the morning. Cassie started at five!

That's another thing about being famous—you have to wake up really, really early.

"How's your butt?" asked Gloria, because she's my best friend and can ask me stuff like that.

"Still sore."

She checked a grid clipped to her board. "Well, according to today's schedule, you're all done cannonballing into the pool. Today you're just a background player."

"Excellent!"

I noticed some paparazzi hanging around in the parking lot behind a rolled-out line of security tape.

"Let's do this thing, man!" Aidan Tyler marched out of his trailer, which was parked pretty close to our neon Welcome to Wonderland sign. It was perfect! Cameras started clicking. Aidan started waving. The Wonderland was in the background of every shot.

"You can't buy that kind of free advertising," said Gloria. "Well, you can. But it would cost a bajillion dollars."

"Did you share Aidan's schedule with the press?" I asked.

Gloria grinned. "Maybe."

We knocked knuckles. Using the movie to market the motel was working, big-time!

"Look!" shouted a guy lugging a video camera. "It's Cassie McGinty with Kevin the Monkey!"

All the other photographers and reporters went wild.

"Kevin!"

"From YouTube!"

"Over here, Kevin!"

Fifty cameras swung away from Aidan to catch the more exciting scene: Cassie with Kevin riding on her shoulder. The monkey was clapping and blowing lip farts. It was hysterical. Luckily, Cassie and Kevin were near our neon sign, too!

"That's so super cute," said Gloria.

I gave her a look. Gloria doesn't usually say girly-girl stuff like "super cute."

"Well, it is!" she said defensively. "It will also ensure maximum media exposure and retweets."

"Yo," said Aidan, smiling and flicking his fingers through his bangs. "Check it out, guys. I'm going to do the Look." He did an over-the-shoulder backward pout.

The cameras clicked and flashed.

At Cassie and Kevin.

"Cassie?" shouted a reporter. "Who's cuter? Aidan or Kevin?"

"It's a toss-up," she answered. "But Kevin's the better kisser."

The monkey puckered up and gave Cassie a wet smack on the cheek. Everybody laughed.

Except Aidan Tyler.

Acting and Reacting

Security guards politely asked the reporters and camerapeople to stay behind the yellow tape as Aidan, Cassie, and Kevin waved good-bye and took their places around the corner at our swimming pool—where the paparazzi couldn't see them.

"Okay, Aidan," said Kurt, ready to set the scene. "This takes place right after Surf Monkey jets around the pool. You're a preppy. Cassie's a hippie. You come from different worlds. But that can't stop Cupid from shooting an arrow straight through your heart. You ready?"

"Yo, I'm the Tyes. I was born ready."

"Perfect. Cassie?"

"All set."

"J.J.?"

"Kevin's ready to rock."

The monkey struck a pose.

"Then let's roll," said Kurt.

The lady with the clapper board marked the scene. The cameras started rolling.

"Aaaaand action!" called Kurt.

"Hello," said Aidan. "I'm Eric Von Wipple. Who. Pray tell. Are you?"

"Cut!" cried Kurt.

"We got it?" asked Aidan.

"No," said Kurt, tugging at the hair on the right side of his head. "It sounds too stilted. Loosen up a little."

"Totally, ace. You got it."

"Take two," said the lady with the clapper board.

"Aaaand action!" said Kurt.

"Yo, hello," said Aidan, his limbs all loose and floppy. "What's shaking, baby? I'm, like, you know, Eric Von Wipple." He flounced toward Cassie. "What do they call you, besides gorgeous?"

"Cut! Give it more energy!"

Woo-hoo. My name is Aidan Tyler. I mean, Eric Von Wipple.

Boing

"Cut!" shouted Kurt, tearing at the hair on the left side of his head.

"We got it?"

"No! Let's do it again. Give it a little more authority."

"You mean like I'm the big boss?"

"Sure," said the director. "Try that."

The clapper board lady slated the scene again.

"Aaaaand action!" said Kurt.

Aidan puffed up his chest. "HELLO!" he barked like a drill sergeant. "I'M ERIC VON WIPPLE. WHO, PRAY TELL, ARE YOU?"

"Cut," sighed Kurt, yanking hair clumps on both sides of his head.

Aidan's two lines would be repeated twenty more times.

Kurt would keep pulling his hair out of his skull.

Because Aidan Tyler was even worse the next twenty times he tried to act.

The Whole World
Is Watching

On take twenty-three, Kurt said, "Try it a little faster, Aidan."

So Aidan did.

"Hello. I'mEricVonWipplewhopraytellareyou?"

On take twenty-four, the director said, "Slow it down."

Aidan did that, too.

"Hellooooo. Iiiiii aaaam Eeeeriiiic Vooooon Wiiiiiiiiiipple."

"Cut!" shouted Kurt. "Cut, cut, cut, cut, cut!"

"Yo?" said Aidan. "We got this or what, man?"

"Um, Kurt?" said Dawg, touching his earpiece. "Just got word: Boris has arrived. He's in Mr. Tyler's trailer."

"Finally," said the director. "Aidan?"

"What?"

He motioned for Aidan to step out of the scene so they could discuss something privately. They moved away from the pool and into the side parking lot.

"Uh-oh," said Gloria. "They're in camera range."

"Not really," I said. "Cassie still is, but Aidan and Kurt aren't. . . ."

"I'm not talking about the movie camera," said Gloria. "I meant those guys."

She nodded toward the pack of press people. Gloria and I hurried over to warn Kurt and Aidan. It was too late.

"We've flown in an acting coach from New York," Kurt told Aidan. "Boris Kolenkov."

"Why, man?"

"He's going to work with you. Help you with your line readings."

"What?" shouted Aidan. "You're cray-cray, Kurt. I don't need no acting coach."

All those photographers behind the yellow tape line? They were merrily shooting Aidan's latest meltdown like mad.

"Bad publicity," Gloria whispered in my ear. "If this goes viral, it could become toxic. People will say *Beach Party Surf Monkey* is a flop long before it even hits a single screen."

She was right. If everybody was saying the movie was a disaster, the money people out in Hollywood might cancel the whole production. And if they did that, Mom might really sell out to Mr. Conch so she could hike in an Arizona desert.

I had to go into damage control mode, pronto!

So while Aidan and Kurt screamed at each other, I strolled over to meet the press as casually as I could. Inside, I was panicking.

"Awesome, isn't it?" I said with a proud smile. "That's Kurt Stroh's famous emotional immersion technique."

"Huh?" said one of the reporters, lowering her camera.

"It's a method Mr. Stroh uses to mine the deep, inner emotions of his cast. Did you catch his musical masterpiece *Put On Your Shoes*? How do you think he got those dancing street urchins to cry like that? I'll tell you." I gestured toward the ugly scene behind me. "Sometimes to build up a character, you need to tear down an actor's emotional walls. Mr. Stroh learned this technique over in Russia, studying with the famous acting teacher Boris Kolenkov, who, as you heard, just arrived here at the Wonderland Motel. I'm curious if he brought any of his other famous clients with him."

"Like who?"

"You know. Bradley, Matt, Leonardo. Jen, Scarlett, Angelina."

"Are they all here?"

I shrugged. "Not sure. But Mr. Kolenkov is very beloved by all his star pupils, most of whom only need first names. I'm just saying they *might* all be here in St. Pete. And since Mr. Kolenkov is Russian, they *might* all be enjoying some early-morning chicken Kiev and herring at the new Russian theme restaurant downtown."

The paparazzi forgot all about Aidan Tyler.

They bolted for their vehicles and took off on my wild Russian goose chase.

As soon as they were gone, Gloria and Dawg

escorted Aidan to his trailer for Acting 101 lessons with the renowned coach from Moscow.

I went over to make sure Cassie was okay.

"You good?"

"Fine. I haven't had to say a word all morning. I just had to wait for Aidan to say his."

"Let's move down to the beach," said the director. "Aidan's not in that scene until the very end."

"Good idea," said Cassie, handing Kevin off to J.J. "Maybe the acting coach can work a minor miracle. Because I hate to say it, but Aidan Tyler is the worst actor I've ever worked with."

"Can you say that louder and with more authority?" I joked, doing my best to sound movie-director-ish.

"AIDAN TYLER IS THE WORST ACTOR I'VE EVER WORKED WITH!"

Everybody on the crew laughed.

"Let's hit the beach," hollered Dawg.

I went to grab my stuff.

When I picked up my towel, I saw Veronica Conch standing on the other side of the fence separating our two properties. She must've been up on a ladder—because the fence is six or seven feet tall.

She waved at me.

I waved back.

She waved again.

I pretended the sun was in my eyes.

Gator Bait

Gloria rejoined Cassie and me down on the beach.

"Excuse me, Cassie," she said, consulting her clipboard. "Do you want the same thing for lunch?"

"Not really," said Cassie.

"Was there something wrong with your smoothie yesterday?"

"No. It was fine. I'd just rather—I don't know— hang out with you guys and have more bologna sandwiches and rippled potato chips. You know—a normal kid lunch."

"That can be arranged," I said. "I'm not too crazy about the world's most wonderful buffet next door."

"So where do you two like to go for fun around here?" asked Cassie.

"Fun food?" said Gloria.

Cassie shook her head. "Just fun."

"Smugglers Cove," I said without missing a beat. "It's an awesome mini golf course on Madeira Beach."

"But you guys have a Putt-Putt golf course right here at the motel," said Cassie, sounding confused.

"True. But I have to be honest: Smugglers Cove is even more awesome. It has a giant pirate ship, a waterfall, and—get this—an alligator feeding station."

"No way."

"Way. You put some grilled chicken on a fishing line and dangle it for the gators to snap down. The first time Grandpa took me, I was maybe in kindergarten. He held me in his arms so I could reach my pole out over the water to feed the biggest alligator, the ornery one they called Ugly Gus, the mean ol' cuss."

I went on. "Well, Ugly Gus chomped down hard on my line and wouldn't let go. But I wouldn't let go of my pole, either. It was a battle of wills. Me against the meanest gator in the swamp."

"You're crazy," said Gloria.

"I prefer the term 'adventurous.'"

"What happened?" asked Cassie.

"That gator yanked me right out of Grandpa's arms! Before I knew it, I was in the swirling water, surrounded by half a dozen agitated alligators who all thought I was the biggest bucket of bait they'd ever seen!"

"What'd you do?" asked Cassie, her eyes wide.

"What everybody should do during an alligator attack. I stayed calm. I didn't splash around. And then I started singing."

"Excuse me?" said Gloria.

"I sang Ugly Gus a song I learned in preschool. Nice and easy. Like a lullaby. 'Alligator, alligator, big and green. You've got the longest tail I've ever seen.' Have you two ever seen an alligator smile?"

"No," said Cassie with a laugh.

"I have. Six of 'em. The more I sang, the more they smiled. Before long, Ugly Gus rolled over and showed me his belly. I scratched it. He purred like a happy kitten. Then he flipped over and let me climb on his back. We rode around the lagoon a couple times, just gliding across the water. Security

guys started yelling at me, so I asked Gus to carry me back to the floating dock where the gators like to sunbathe. I reminded them all to use sunblock while somebody lowered a ladder, and I climbed back to Grandpa."

I opened my wallet, where I keep mostly coupons and cards.

"And that's why, to this very day, I still have a free pass to Smugglers Cove. They gave it to me so we wouldn't sue them, I guess. But now I can play Putt-Putt anytime I want. I just can't feed the alligators anymore."

"That is so cool," said Cassie.

"Here," I said, handing her the free pass. "Use it sometime while you're in town. And tell Ugly Gus that P. T. Wilkie says hi."

Gloria cleared her throat. "Correct me if I'm wrong, P.T., but don't all the merchants up and down the beaches give free passes to all the motel operators in hopes that you will promote their attractions to guests?"

"Maybe," I said.

"I don't care," said Cassie. "I like P.T.'s story better."

"Yeah," said Gloria. "Me too."

Hitting the Beach!

The crew had been setting up cameras, lights, scenery, and props on the beach since before the sun popped up.

That sort of activity will draw a crowd. I'd say maybe two hundred curious onlookers were lined up behind a banner of rolled-out tape. Some new photographers were there, too.

"This is so cool," said Pinky. "Look at all those people."

Veronica Conch was in the crowd, cradling one of those yappy little foo-foo dogs in her arms. She waved.

I waved back.

She waved again.

I pretended the sun was in my eyes. Again.

The scene we were about to film was another

big dance number. I was back to playing a finger-snapping blob in the background. But I knew there might be a chance I could get upgraded again, so I was going to be the best blob I possibly could!

Gunther, the German director of photography, wanted to wait for what he kept calling *goldene Zeit,* which I found out meant "golden time"—the moment the morning sun would be at the perfect angle to make the beach look fantastic.

"It will be a very short window, folks," announced Dawg. "So let's get it right on the first take."

Since Aidan Tyler wasn't in the scene, we had a chance of actually doing that.

"Goldene Zeit!" shouted Gunther, pointing at the sun.

"You all set?" the director asked Cassie.

"Yes, sir!"

J.J. handed Kevin to Cassie. The monkey scampered up to her shoulder.

"Roll playback," said the director.

"Roll playback," shouted Dawg.

"Rolling playback," said the soundman, tapping a button.

And that's when everything went bananas.

More Fun Than a Barrel of Monkeys

Wild guitar riffs blasted.

Dancers gyrated.

Kevin the Monkey bopped to the beat.

Cassie and the chorus lip-synched to the lyrics.

"Hey there, ho there, Mr. Sun is gonna shine.
Time for makin' waves and feelin' fine.
Surf's up! (Go, Surf Monkey!)
Surf's up! (Go, Surf Monkey!)—"

All of a sudden, Veronica Conch's little foo-foo dog started yapping something fierce.

"Cut!" shouted Kurt.

The music skidded to a warbly, ear-piercingly harsh halt—totally terrifying the terrier.

The little dog leapt out of Veronica's arms and charged across the beach, its tiny legs churning up a sandstorm. It was yipping and yapping and gunning for what it figured was the source of the horrible noise: Kevin the Monkey.

Kevin saw the dog and scampered up to perch on top of Cassie McGinty's 1960s beehive hairdo. He stood up and thumped his chest like he was King Kong.

That only made the dog nuttier. It snarled and let loose a barrage of barks.

First Kevin shrieked and then he freaked.

He leapt off Cassie's head, hit the sand, and took off.

"Kevin!" shouted J.J. "Come back."

"Fluffy!" shouted Veronica. "Heel."

"Goldene Zeit!" shouted Gunther.

There was a whole lot of shouting going on.

"Arrest that monkey!" Veronica hollered.

"Control your dog!" screamed J.J.

"It's not my dog, lady!" shouted Veronica. "I'm pet-sitting!"

I was watching the chase scene from where the surf hits the sand, because that's where we background actors were positioned for the big dance number.

"We have lost zee golden light!" Gunther sobbed behind the camera.

Kurt threw up his arms. "This is a disaster!"

I had to agree. Totally.

"You people never should've made this movie here!" Veronica Conch shouted over her shoulder.

"I agree," muttered the director.

We were doomed! Even the neighborhood dogs were trying to destroy the Wonderland's chance at becoming the most famous motel in Florida.

But then I had an idea.

I remembered something the animal trainer had told me one day when I was watching Kevin rehearse: "Monkeys feel safest up high. They love trees."

I tore across the beach, which, by the way, is extremely hard to do unless you're on the wet part, like I was.

So while J.J. and Veronica slipped and slid across the sand, I ran. I also called Grandpa.

"Hello?" he said, sounding kind of groggy. I must've woken him up from his early-morning nap.

"Grandpa," I panted.

"P.T.? Why are you breathing so hard? You should see a doctor. . . ."

"Meet . . . me . . . behind . . . the . . . Sea . . . Spray . . . Motel."

"Why?"

"Kevin . . . the . . . Monkey. Running . . . for . . . trees. Sea . . . Spray. Hurry. Bring . . . bologna!"

Bologna: The Duct Tape of Foods

I was right.

Fluffy the dog treed Kevin the Monkey behind the Sea Spray Motel. Turned out it was an orange tree. I learned this when Kevin hurled a few juicy fruit bombs down at Fluffy.

"Sit," I said to Fluffy, since I was the first to arrive on the scene.

Fluffy didn't sit. Instead, he snarled. At me.

"That monkey is a menace!" said Veronica Conch, huffing and puffing her way up the sandy slope to join me at the base of the tree.

"Heads up!" I shouted.

Kevin had just launched another rotten orange.

It bonked Veronica in the head.

"Ouch!" whined Veronica. Hot orange juice,

Orange juice. It's not just for breakfast anymore.

SPLAT!

seeds, and pulp dribbled down around her ears. "That's assault and battery!"

"Your dog started it," said J.J., who'd finally reached the orange grove. She was followed by several of the gawkers, who found the dog-monkey chase more exciting than the stalled dance scene on the beach.

"For the last time," said Veronica, "Fluffy is not my dog. I am pet-sitting for a guest, because unlike some fly-by-night operations, the Conch Reef Resort is a full-service hotel, which is why you guys should've made this movie at our place instead of the Blunderland!"

Veronica yanked Fluffy off the ground and squeezed his wiggling body against her chest. "Quit. Squirming. Dog."

"Why aren't you in school?" I asked.

"Because!" was Veronica's answer.

"What's our situation?" asked Gloria, joining us under the tree with her clipboard and radio.

"Kevin's scared but he's safe," said J.J.

"He'd be safer over at our resort!" snapped Veronica. "We have security guards and much stricter leash rules than the Wonderland, which, hello, isn't even a hotel. It's a *mo*tel!"

Gloria ignored her. "Kevin is fine," she relayed to whoever was on the other end of her walkie-talkie.

"But now comes the hard part," said J.J. "Coaxing him down."

"Yeah," snorted Veronica. "Good luck with that!"

J.J. started making clicking noises with her tongue.

Kevin looked down at her like he thought she was an idiot. No way was he falling for the old "clicking my tongue to make you think I'm a monkey" trick.

Finally, Grandpa arrived on the scene.

"Step aside, coming through," he said to part the crowd. "Emergency bologna delivery."

"Bologna?" Veronica said with a laugh. "What are you gonna do with bologna, old man?"

Grandpa ignored Veronica, too. He handed me a sealed package of Oscar Mayer's finest circular luncheon meat.

"Is that really bologna?" said J.J.

I nodded. "It has a very strong odor. A lot of animals can't resist the scent."

J.J. arched an eyebrow. "And if I may ask, where did you learn this interesting piece of animal trivia?"

"Working with the tigers at Wild Cat Safariland over in Tampa." (Actually, it was more like I was running away from them.)

"Liar!" shouted Veronica. "That's just another one of your silly stories!"

It was my turn to ignore her. I peeled back the plastic wrapper.

The spicy, hot-doggish aroma of processed pork whacked my nostrils hard.

It whacked Kevin's even harder.

He hesitated for half a second, then scurried down the tree trunk.

I handed the bologna to J.J. The monkey leapt into her arms. She gave him a few tasty bites.

"The cat is in the bag," Gloria said to her walkie-talkie. "The monkey is on the merry-go-round."

"Huh?" somebody squawked through the tinny speaker.

"Sorry," she said. "Kevin the Monkey is fine and headed back to the set with J.J."

Grandpa proudly displayed his package of luncheon meat to the crowd. "Bologna, ladies and gentlemen. It is the duct tape of foods. There ain't nothing it can't do!"

Surf's Back Up!

Ten minutes later, we were once again ready to shoot the big dance number.

"The sun is still nearly perfect," announced Gunther. "But we must hurry! *Mach schnell!*"

Cassie's hair was back to looking like a bubbly beehive instead of a monkey-clawed rat's nest. Kevin the Monkey was totally chill, pecking a piece of bologna out of Grandpa's hand. Veronica had taken the yappy dog back to its owners.

Everything was as it should be.

"All right, everybody," said Kurt through his megaphone. "Let's take it from the top!"

"Let's take it from the top!" hollered Dawg, scanning the crowd of spectators, looking for potential disasters.

The lady with the slate slapped it shut. "Scene nine hundred, take two!"

"Aaaaand action!" shouted Kurt.

The music started up again.

So did the dancing.

I didn't have to "act" or pretend that I was excited. The scene was one of the most spectacular things I've ever seen!

And Pinky Nelligan?

The guy can dance almost as good as he sings.

Waves are crashing, Surf Monkey's smashing, jellyfish are dashing, here comes some splashing!

On a cue from his trainer, Surf Monkey puckered his lips as if he were whistling.

Two hippie girls ran down the beach with a monkey-sized surfboard. It had an upright handlebar like you'd see on a scooter.

Kevin hoisted his mini surfboard over his head and dashed toward the waves.

When he reached the waterline, the director called, "Cut!"

The monkey froze.

"Good boy!" shouted J.J. "Mr. Wilkie?"

"More bologna," cried Grandpa, shuffling across the sand. "Coming through!"

Yep. Grandpa had another fun new job: Assistant Animal Trainer in Charge of Meat Treats.

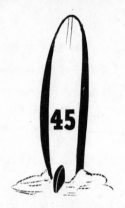

Test Drive

"**M**an, he loves that bologna more than any reward I've ever given him!" I heard J.J. say.

Grandpa shrugged. "He has good taste. Same as me."

"You want to test the rig while we're here?" J.J. asked the director when he was happy with the song and dance number after only two takes.

"Good idea."

Suddenly, we heard Aidan Tyler screaming, way up at the motel.

"Scram, man! I don't need no acting coach."

"Pah!" boomed a voice with a Russian accent. "There is nothing more I, Boris Kolenkov, can do. You have the emotional range of a turtle!"

"Takes one to know one!" Aidan was in full meltdown mode.

So naturally, cameras were clicking. Phones were up and shooting videos. Another Aidan Tyler temper tantrum was being live-tweeted and I was too far away to stop it.

Kurt rolled his eyes. "We're going to be down here all night shooting Aidan's next two lines. Let's hurry up and test the monkey gag while we still have a chance."

Dawg barked orders into his walkie-talkie while the prop guys carried in a second surfboard that looked exactly like the one Kevin the Monkey had been toting over his head. Only, this new board had a remote-controled submarine with propellers attached to its bottom.

Kevin rode on J.J.'s shoulder as the trainer waded into the water.

"You ready to rock?" she asked the monkey. She said that a lot. I think it was a cue for Kevin to focus.

I started wishing that we had an Aidan Tyler trainer, too.

Kevin took his place on the surfboard. J.J. strapped him into a life jacket. Two motorized skiffs were set to shadow the monkey's moves.

"Give it a go," said the director when everything was ready. "Hurry."

On the beach, one of the special effects guys thumbed a remote control. Surf Monkey slid across the water. J.J. hollered a couple of different commands. Kevin raised one hand over his head, executed a backflip, did a butt-wiggle dance. He reminded me of Grandpa doing the Swim.

He was so hysterical the paparazzi stopped focusing on Aidan Tyler and turned their lenses on Kevin the Monkey!

Everybody cheered, which made Kevin act even goofier.

He flipped over the handlebar, dipped his toes in the water to hang ten, and flashed us all a big smile as he zoomed by.

The crowd went crazy!

"Aiyyo? What y'all doin' with that mangy monkey, man?"

Aidan Tyler was back on the set.

He did not look or sound happy.

Wiggy for a Piggy

"**A**re you fools almost done monkeying around or what?" demanded Aidan, flanked by his flunkies.

They all made pouty faces whenever their star made a pouty face, to let us know they were just as upset as Aidan was.

"Why'd you even call me to the set, man? I could be in my trailer, chillaxin'."

"We were using the downtime between shots to test the Surf Monkey rig," explained Kurt. "You were supposed to use this time to work with Mr. Kolenkov."

"Forget that noise. I don't need no acting coach. I'm Aidan Tyler! I'm a superstar!"

J.J. and the props guys brought Kevin the Monkey and his tricked-out surfboard back to shore.

I don't need no grammar coach, neither!

Aidan and his entire entourage crossed their arms over their chests and frowned.

"Okay," said the director. "Let's stow the surfboard rig. We're ready to start shooting your scene, Aidan. This is where you flirt with Polly Pureheart on the beach."

"Not if she has that fool monkey."

"What?"

"I'm Aidan Tyler. The Tyes. I need to keep it real, man."

His minions nodded.

"No way would I fall for a girl who hangs around

with a funky monkey. Besides, Kevin the Monkey ain't the right costar for me in this movie."

"What?" The director started tugging at both sides of his hair again.

"Monkeys are so last year, man. This is the year of the pig."

"What?"

Aidan had reduced the director's vocabulary to one word.

"See, while I was hangin' in my trailer, before the Russkie dude showed up, I did me some Googling, man. You ever check out Porker D. Pigg's YouTube channel?"

"Um, no . . ."

"Yo—Porker is the fo' rizzle pigizzle."

"You're joking," said Cassie. "Two days into the shoot, you seriously want to replace Kevin the Monkey with some pig?"

"Yo, Cee McG. This isn't 'some pig.' This is Porker D. Pigg. Hashtag shakin' bacon."

"So," said Cassie, keeping cool, "you think we should basically change the whole script and call our movie *Beach Party Surf Pig*?"

"Exactly!" said Aidan. "Now you're seeing the big picture, girl. The movie poster would be off the chain!

"And," he added, "we should change locations."

"Excuse me?" I said, because, hello, *Beach Party*

Surf Monkey was supposed to make the Wonder-land so famous nobody would dare tear it down, not even Mr. Edward Conch. Changing locations would mean that would never happen.

"We should film this movie in Iowa," Aidan said. "It's pig heaven."

"It's a beach movie!" shouted Cassie.

"So? Don't they have beaches in Iowa?"

"No," said Cassie. "They have cornfields!"

"Corn is cool."

When Aidan said that, Cassie convulsed with laughter.

Me? I didn't find it so funny. If the movie moved

to Iowa, our rooms would all be empty. We'd be broke. Mom would definitely snag Mr. Conch's offer to buy us out. We'd have to find a new home.

Which meant I might be moving to Iowa, too.

Or Arizona.

It didn't really matter where. It wouldn't be the Wonderland.

Monkey See, Monkey Doo

"I just figured this out!" said Cassie. "You're jealous! Of a monkey! You're afraid Kevin will get more laughs than you!"

"He's already a better actor," muttered Kurt.

"That scrawny, bug-eyed loser?" snarled Aidan. "You think I'm jealous of *him*? Ha!"

"Mr. Tyler?" said Gloria. "Let's try to remain professional. . . ."

Aidan ignored her, dug some kind of bright green wristband out of his pocket, and stretched it between his forefinger and thumb.

"I want that monkey out of my movie!" he said. "Pronto, if not sooner."

"*Your* movie?" said Cassie.

"You and Miss McGinty are costars," said Gloria diplomatically.

"No way, gofer girl. Check the stats. I'm a way bigger star than Cee McG and Mr. Monkey combined. So get him outta here!"

Aidan aimed his rubber band pistol at Kevin and let it fly.

Kevin screeched and ducked.

The wristband missed. Barely.

"Hey," said J.J. "Don't you ever do that again, Mr. Tyler."

"Or what? You're gonna fire me, monkey woman?"

Gloria unclipped her walkie-talkie. "Ms. Foxworth?" she said into her radio mic. "We need you on set. ASAP."

"Dawn Foxworth don't scare me, man. I'm Aidan Tyler. I'm the Tyes. Can't nobody tell me what to do. Hey, Cee McG? They ever make a lunch box out of your face, girl? How about a backpack? Your face on a backpack? Mine is!"

"Mr. Tyler," said Gloria, "let's not say anything we might regret later."

She was trying to calm Aidan down, which is sort of like asking a hurricane to behave like a nice tropical breeze.

"What's the problem?" asked Ms. Foxworth as she marched down to the beach.

"Same old, same old," said Kurt, tossing up his hands. "Aidan is throwing another hissy fit."

"Yo, this flunky monkey is ruining my movie!" said Aidan. "I want him fired!"

That was when Kevin hopped off J.J.'s shoulder, squatted in the sand, and did something most monkeys do on a regular basis.

He pooped.

And then he did something a few zoo monkeys do when they don't like the people gawking at them in their cages.

He scooped up his poop into a ball and hurled it—straight at Aidan Tyler!

Monkeyshines

*S*plat!

Aidan Tyler's pink polo shirt was covered with a stinky brown mess.

Splat!

So was his face.

Kevin the Monkey chuckled.

Fact: you should never fling things at monkeys. They might fling back.

Everybody else sort of grinned, including a lot of the spectators standing behind the rolled-out yellow security tape. People held up their phones to take more pictures. I predicted a new hashtag was about to start trending on Instagram: #AidanIsAPoopyHead.

"That monkey disrespected me!" whined Aidan,

wiping gunk off his face. "You need to fire him, Ms. Foxworth! He attacked me, man!"

"You attacked him first!" said the trainer.

"So? I can do whatever I want! I'm a major celebrity!"

"Actually," said Cassie, "right now you're nothing but a big baby."

"Oooh!" said all nine of Aidan's flunkies.

"Now *you're* disrespectin' me, too? That cuts deep, Cee McG. Real deep."

"Cassie?" said Ms. Foxworth. "Why don't you go to your trailer?"

"Because, unfortunately, Aidan and I have a scene to shoot."

"Yo!" said Aidan. "I got monkey stink all over me. I ain't shootin' nothin' till y'all dump this nasty mongrel monkey and sign on Porker D. Pigg! And remember: I've got a national concert tour starting in two weeks."

"We be bouncin' in fourteen days," said one of Aidan's hangers-on. I think it was the guy who carried his breath mints.

"Aidan?" said Ms. Foxworth.

"What?"

"Why don't you go clean yourself up? Put on a fresh shirt."

"A'ight. But y'all are gonna check out Porker, right?"

The producer nodded. "We will definitely take your suggestion under consideration."

"What?" said Cassie. "I am not doing *Beach Party Surf Pig*. If Kevin the Monkey isn't in the movie, neither am I. I'll quit!"

"Cassie?" said the producer. "Why don't you wait in your trailer?"

"Because I—"

"Cassie?"

Her shoulders sank. "Yes, Mom."

Mom?

Plot Twists

Was the movie's executive producer, Dawn Fox-worth, really Cassie McGinty's mother?

I looked at Gloria. She shrugged. She didn't have a clue, either. We needed to do some more McGinty research after we wrapped for the day.

That came sooner than either one of us expected.

Cassie went to her trailer. Aidan went to his. Kevin and J.J. went to their room.

"That's a wrap for today, everybody," announced Dawg. "We'll send out call sheets for tomorrow morning later tonight." And then he muttered, "Once we know if our monkey is turning into a pig . . ."

Gloria and I headed up to the Wonderland.

When we reached the shuffleboard court, Veronica Conch was there, smiling smugly.

"Hi, guys," she said. "Too bad your movie's totally falling apart."

"It's not falling apart," I said.

"Just a few minor bumps in the road," added Gloria.

Veronica laughed. "Yeah. Right. Anyway, this is where Daddy and I think we should put the big bend in our lazy river."

"Your what?"

"Our lazy river. It'll wind from our swimming pool on the other side of the fence, make a big turn here, and head back to the original Conch Reef Resort. I'm thinking floating under a waterfall would be cool, too. We could put one right there, where you have the stupid jackalope statue."

"For the last time," I said, "we are not selling our motel to your father so he can tear it down and put in a lazy river or a Jacuzzi lounge."

"Yes, you are. Right before you go bankrupt, which I predict will happen pretty darn soon, since, oops, you kicked out all your regular guests to make room for the movie people and now they're going to leave, too. I hear Aidan wants to go to Iowa. I read about it on his Facebook page."

"Nobody is leaving," said Gloria. "The production company signed contracts. . . ."

"Yeah. Right. Don't you guys know anything about Hollywood? They'll weasel out of your deal faster than you can say 'green screen.' They're all phonies living in a world of make-believe. They kind of remind me of you, P.T., and all your silly tall tales. I've never understood why my father thinks you're so super special. 'Oh, that P. T. Wilkie is such a genius. He reminds me of me. Always coming up with new ways to make money.' Blah-blah-blah."

It was weird, but for half a second, that made me feel good. "He says that kind of stuff? About me?"

"Ever since we moved in! I guess your own father doesn't think you're all that hot, though. I've never even seen him around!"

Okay. That hurt. Little bit.

"Take a hike, sister," said Gloria.

"What?"

"Go home. This shuffleboard court is the exclusive property of the Wonderland Motel, solely intended for the private use and enjoyment of registered guests."

"Fine. Whatever. But guess what? Pretty soon these shuffleboard courts are going to be a lazy river and I'll be the one kicking you guys off *my* private property!"

And Now the News

Later Gloria and I did all sorts of research on Cassie McGinty and Ms. Foxworth.

We were using the computer in our business center.

Actually, it's just a table we have set up in the corner of the lobby with a coffeepot, a clunky old computer, and a printer. Not many businesspeople stay at the Wonderland, except, of course, Gloria.

"Wow," said Gloria. "We should have dug a little deeper when we did our initial data dive."

"Why? We were only interested in Cassie McGinty the movie star—not Cassie McGinty the real person."

Dawn Foxworth *was* Cassie McGinty's mother.

"I think it's sweet that Cassie and her mother work together," said Mom. She was behind the counter, running numbers through her calculator and projecting how much money we'd lose if the movie people bailed on us.

Short answer? A ton!

"Uh, Mom?" I said. "Can you turn that up?"

Aidan Tyler's horrified face filled the TV set behind our front desk. There was a, uh, mud stain on his polo shirt. Apparently, *Access Hollywood* had obtained "Exclusive Footage of Florida *Beach Party* Meltdown."

"What a major moviemaking mess in Florida," said the anchorwoman. "Literally. We're talking monkey-poop messy, Bob!"

"That's right, Buffy," said Bob. "Teen heartthrob Aidan Tyler wants to fire his dung-flinging costar, Kevin the Monkey."

"But," said Buffy, "Academy Award winner Cassie McGinty is threatening to walk off the set if the monkey's not in the picture."

Then they cut to video footage of Cassie.

"If Kevin the Monkey isn't in the movie," she told the whole world, "neither am I. I'll quit!"

"Wow," said Buffy with a chuckle. "Things certainly are heating up in Florida—and this time, sunshine has nothing to do with it."

Mom snapped off the TV set.

Mr. Ortega came into the lobby, decked out in his snazzy sportscaster blazer.

"Oh, hi, Manny," said Mom. She sounded so bummed. She didn't even bother fluffing up her hair or taking off her glasses.

"Hiya, Wanda. Hiya, kids." He flashed us his smile. I think Mr. Ortega might have LEDs in his teeth. "I'm on my way to the studio to prep the eleven o'clock sportscast." He jabbed a thumb at the darkened TV screen. "Sorry about this PR nightmare."

"The movie people may leave," said Mom sadly. "Mr. Conch's offer is looking better and better all the time. If we sell out, Manny, we'll try to give you guys at least a two-week notice."

"Thank you, Wanda. We'd appreciate it. Of course, we'd appreciate you staying in business even more." He leaned on the counter. "I like it here."

Mom leaned on the counter and sighed. It was different from her usual sighs. This one sounded happy instead of sad.

"I like it here, too," said Mom.

Finally, she took off her glasses.

"Gloria?" said Mr. Ortega when he and Mom finally broke out of their trance.

"Yes, Dad?"

"While I'm away . . ."

"I'll stay safe and ask Ms. Wilkie for permission before P.T. and I do anything crazy like chase after jewel thieves again."

"That's my girl. Watch me at eleven. We'll have highlights and scores from all the big games!"

He gave us a two-finger salute off his cocked eyebrow and headed out the door.

Mom did another happy sigh, watching him go.

But her happy didn't last for long.

The next morning, Kevin the Monkey was gone.

Lost Monkey

"**H**e's gone!" shouted J.J. as she banged the bell on our front desk first thing in the morning.

Seriously. It was like six a.m. The monkey trainer was in the lobby, frantic because Kevin was missing. Mom and I were still in our pajamas.

"I had the screen down and the window open," J.J. said, sort of hyperventilating. "Just two or three inches. I've done it every night since we first checked in. Kevin likes a breeze."

"Don't you keep him in a cage?" asked Mom.

"Of course not. Cages are cruel!"

"Could he squeeze through an opening that small?" I asked.

J.J. nodded. "He must've squirmed under the window, punched a hole through the screen, and taken off."

"Why?" asked Mom.

"I have no idea. He was having so much fun. Making people laugh, making a movie—it was all a game for him. Except when Aidan Tyler was mean to him, of course. . . ."

Mom took off her glasses and rubbed the bridge of her nose. Now her brow was furrowed so deep she could plant banana trees up there.

Losing the monkey meant we were inching closer to losing the movie. Cassie's TV clip kept running through my head: *If Kevin the Monkey isn't in the movie, neither am I. I'll quit!*

"He could get hurt!" said J.J. "If he tries to cross the street, it could be even worse!"

Mom called the police.

I texted Gloria. She was already awake, watching some TV show about the stock market in Japan. She texted back:

OMW.

"Don't worry, guys," I told Mom and J.J. "We'll find Kevin. I promise."

Gloria and I avoided the predawn paparazzi hanging out in the parking lot—sipping coffee and waiting for the next big Hollywood scandal—and slipped around back to examine the area near the window our favorite monkey had escaped through.

"We might be able to find some tracks in the flower bed," I told Gloria. "Maybe some paw prints on the sidewalk. Something that might help us figure out which way he went."

We both turned on the flashlight apps in our phones and began searching for clues.

"We probably shouldn't touch anything until the cops show up," I said, because I watch a lot of those *CSI* shows and am, therefore, an expert on forensics.

I noticed that the hibiscus bush underneath the window was dented and sort of wedged open. I figured that's where Kevin landed when he jumped out of the window. The impact pushed the branches apart.

"You two find anything?" asked Grandpa, who was up super early, especially for him. "J.J. is walking around, clicking her tongue at trees. She told me Kevin ran away."

"We're trying to figure out which way he went," said Gloria.

"I see shoe prints," I said, staring down at the Bermuda grass. "But no monkey paw prints."

"Maybe Kevin put on sneakers to sneak away!" said Grandpa.

Fact: he doesn't watch as many *CSI* shows as I do.

52

CSI: St. Pete Beach

"If Kevin ran away," I wondered aloud, "why aren't there any paw prints?"

"I was wondering the same thing," said Gloria.

The fast-rising sun glinted off the sparkly stuff in the flower beds—crushed seashells Grandpa sprinkles around to "give the place pizzazz."

I also noticed a slight circular stain on the window-sill. A dark spot. Probably because when Grandpa's doing touch-ups around the motel, he has a bad habit of setting his paint can down on a section he's just finished painting. That'll leave a circle. Most of our stucco looks a little spotty.

And of course, there was a huge hole punched through the window screen—from inside.

Since we still didn't have a clue as to which way Kevin went, we headed back to the lobby to try to

figure out what we should do next. Two police officers were there, talking to Mom and J.J.

"We're both big Kevin the Monkey fans," said one.

"Huge," said the other. "Love his YouTube
channel."

"Remember when he did that backward basketball toss? Nothing but net!"

They both laughed and munched on doughnuts
from our breakfast buffet.

"But this really isn't a crime," said one. "Not yet,
anyway."

Smudges on window glass? Did someone forget to wash this window last weekend before the guests checked in? Was that someone me? Why aren't there any paw prints? Can Kevin the Monkey fly like those monkeys in <u>The Wizard of Oz</u>?

Impact crater from monkey jump

"You folks should hang up some posters," suggested the second officer. "Like people do when they lose a dog or cat."

"Maybe you could drive around, calling his name," suggested her partner. "You know, 'Kevin? Here, boy! Kevin? Where are you?' Stuff like that."

When they were all out of suggestions, the two officers drove away in their police cruiser. They didn't even turn on the sirens. Sirens would've been cool.

Next door, the Conch Reef Resort had a new message on its splashy illuminated sign:

● ● ● ● ● ● ● ● ● ● ● ● ● ● ● ● ●

COMING SOON: THE ALL-NEW
LAZY RIVER!
FREE INNER TUBES!

● ● ● ● ● ● ● ● ● ● ● ● ● ● ● ● ●

In my mind, I could already hear the bulldozers revving their engines.

Gloria went to an emergency production meeting with Ms. Foxworth, Kurt, Dawg, and the heads of all the different crew departments.

"So?" I asked her when the meeting finally broke up.

"I told them my dad and the folks at WTSP would help us search for Kevin."

"Cool. What about the movie? Can they still make *Beach Party Surf Monkey* without the monkey? Or does Mom have to go ahead and sell our motel to Mr. Conch?"

"They'll rearrange the schedule," said Gloria. "Shoot all the non-monkey scenes they can. Kurt says they can film without Kevin for a day or two. But eventually, if we can't find him, they'll have to circle back and make a tough market-driven decision."

"What do you mean?" I asked, even though I probably didn't want to hear the answer.

"*Beach Party Surf Monkey* or *Beach Party Surf Pig.*"

"You're kidding. Cassie said she'd never do the movie with a pig."

"Her mom says Cassie might reconsider. Porker will arrive from Iowa this afternoon. Aidan Tyler just sent his private jet to pick him up."

Fact: when you're famous, like Aidan Tyler, anything's possible.

You can even make pigs fly.

Code Banana Yellow

This was worse than a nightmare.

At least during a nightmare you can punch your pillow.

The monkey hunt was in full swing up and down St. Pete Beach.

Taking the police officers' suggestion, I printed a stack of Lost Monkey posters and taped them everywhere I could. Poles, store windows—I even tucked them under windshield wipers.

J.J. and the Sunshine State Primate Sanctuary

REWARD!

Last seen at the
Wonderland motel
Starring in a major
motion picture

offered a ten-thousand-dollar reward, which was noted on the poster as well as on Kevin the Monkey's official Facebook page and Twitter feed. They drove around in their van, searching for him.

Mr. Ortega did a live remote broadcast from the parking lot of the IHOP down the street, because our parking lot was full of trucks, campers, and RVs for the movie stars and crew.

"We're issuing a code banana yellow," Mr. Ortega told his midmorning TV viewers. "If you see Kevin the Monkey, we urge you to call the WTSP hotline, the ASPCA, or your local police. Do not attempt to apprehend the monkey yourself. If you do, he might hurl something at you—something that could potentially stain your garments. So let's leave the monkey rescue to the trained professionals, folks. But if you monkey see, please monkey do call the number at the bottom of your screen. . . ."

Gloria was back at the Wonderland with the crew. At ten a.m., they started shooting scenes that didn't need Kevin the Monkey. I texted her.

HOW'S IT GOING?

OK. PINKY JUST SANG A SOLO LINE. AIDAN MADE KURT CUT IT.

WHY?

PINKY SINGS BETTER. ACTS BETTER, TOO.
AIDAN HATES WHEN THAT HAPPENS.

I made my way back up Gulf Boulevard toward the Wonderland, figuring we'd done all we could.

The posters were everywhere.

The local radio stations had picked up Mr. Ortega's "code banana yellow" and were broadcasting information about the "missing monkey movie star."

I was sure somebody would spot Kevin. Soon. Besides, according to the revised daily schedule, I was supposed to be in another crowd scene after the lunch break. They needed my elbow in the background.

But I froze in front of the Wonderland when I saw a great inflatable ape anchored beside the Conch Reef Resort's video-screen billboard. The monkey balloon was bigger than the one we'd rented for the tram tours. This one looked big enough to star in the Macy's Thanksgiving Day Parade.

Colorful titles flashed in on the screen:

• • • • • • • • • • • • • • • •
**GETTING HUNGRY SEARCHING FOR
KEVIN THE MONKEY?
COME IN AND TRY OUR WORLD-CLASS
ONE-OF-A-KIND STUFFED BANANA
PANCAKES AT OUR ALL-NEW ALL-DAY
BREAKFAST BUFFET!**
• • • • • • • • • • • • • • • •

Then, believe it or not, the flashing type was replaced by a slick video clip of Aidan Tyler looking over his shoulder and winking at the camera while a caption scrolled across the bottom of the screen:

● ● ● ● ● ● ● ● ● ● ● ● ● ● ● ● ● ● ●

**TAKE IT FROM AIDAN TYLER:
AT THE CONCH REEF RESORT,
THEY DON'T MONKEY AROUND!
LOOK FOR OUR NEW JACUZZI LOUNGE
AND EXPANDED PARKING
OPPORTUNITIES RIGHT NEXT DOOR—
COMING SOON!**

● ● ● ● ● ● ● ● ● ● ● ● ● ● ● ● ● ● ●

While I stood there gawking, Grandpa drifted out to the parking lot, shaking his head.

His eyes were moist. I'm pretty sure if I hadn't been there, he would've cried.

"Edward Conch has the flashy celebrities and megabucks," he said, sounding defeated. "It's Disney World all over again!"

Can Things Get Any Worse?

We kept shooting scenes without Kevin the Monkey.

Me and my elbows kept being in the background.

And just like Gloria had texted me, Aidan Tyler was really getting super jealous of Pinky Nelligan.

"Aiyyo, that kid should go back to middle school and sing in the choir," he told Kurt and Ms. Foxworth.

Pinky? You stinky! And I saw you touching my M&M's, man. You put those blue ones in there again, didn't you?

"You fools need to fire that choirboy," demanded Aidan. "Otherwise, I'm out!"

Great. I was the one who'd suggested that Pinky be in the movie. Now they were going to fire him?

"I'm sorry," the director told Pinky. "But I have to keep Aidan happy."

"I understand," said Pinky. "It was a pleasure working with you, sir."

What can I say? Pinky's a classy guy. A real pro (even though he's a total amateur).

"I'm sorry," I told him after he turned in his costume.

"Totally unfair," added Gloria.

Pinky shrugged. "Hey, it was fun—now it's done. Good luck, guys. You're going to need it."

"We definitely are," said Gloria as Pinky headed home.

"What do you mean?" I asked.

"Pretty soon we need to shoot monkey scenes, P.T. We can't keep shooting around Kevin. . . ."

"But Kevin's still missing."

"Obviously. That's why we have to bite the bullet and take the hit."

"What bullet and hit are we talking about here?"

"Porker D. Pigg. Kurt is ready to reshoot the two big scenes we shot with Kevin."

"I still don't think Cassie will do it," I said.

"She might."

"Is her mother going to make her?"

"Well, Ms. Foxworth and I were kind of hoping *you* could convince her."

"Me?"

"Cassie likes you. Plus, you and your family have the most at stake here, P.T. If she won't finish the shoot with Surf Pig instead of Surf Monkey, the whole production will most likely shut down."

"Our rooms will all be empty."

Gloria nodded.

"We'll be broke."

Gloria nodded again.

"Mom will sell to Mr. Conch. Grandpa will be bummed."

Gloria gave me one more nod.

"The pig is here?" I asked.

"Just arrived. He's standing by, poolside."

I took in a deep breath. "Where's Cassie?"

"In her trailer."

"Okay."

Now it was time for *me* to put lipstick on a pig.

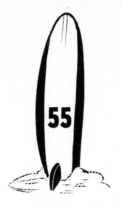

Trailer Talk

I went around to the front parking lot and knocked on the rattly aluminum door to Cassie McGinty's Winnebago.

"Who is it?"

"P. T. Wilkie."

"Did you bring bologna sandwiches?"

"No. But I could go—"

She laughed. "Come on in."

I climbed up the short set of steps.

Cassie was sitting on a couch reading a movie script—for a different movie.

"Hi," I said.

"Hey. What's up? Did they find Kevin?"

"Not yet."

"Well, it's only been like eight hours. . . ."

"I know. Can I talk to you?"

"Sure. Grab a seat."

I sat down in the swivel chair across from the couch and started babbling.

"Well, uh . . . you know . . . I . . . that is, we . . . or mostly me . . . that is, I . . ."

For maybe the first time in my life, I didn't know what to say. I thought about telling a story about three little pigs who each built a motel and mine would be the one built out of straw, because a big bad wolf named Mr. Conch was about to come along and blow it all down.

"Is this about the pig?" said Cassie.

"Yeah. I know you don't want to make the movie with Porker."

"Did my mother send you in here?"

"No. I'm doing this for *my* mom. And me. And Grandpa. See, we pinned the whole entire future of our motel on this one movie. All our regular guests checked out. The place next door is doing all the wacky stunts we used to do. If you guys leave, we'll be in big, big trouble."

"And if I do a bad movie, my career might be in big, big trouble."

"I know."

"Nobody will hire me. I might not be famous anymore."

I nodded. "True."

"I might have to lead a normal life and go to a normal school and eat normal lunches."

I gave her a grin. "Bologna, mustard, and white bread."

Now she started to smile. "With rippled potato chips."

"And pickles."

"No, pickle relish."

She stood up. Grabbed her sunglasses. "So, where's this pig?"

"Out by the pool."

"Well, come on, P.T. We don't want to keep my new costar waiting."

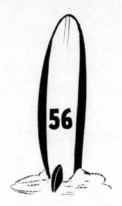

Beach Party Surf Pig!

Since we were reshooting the pool scene where Surf Monkey raced around on his Jet Ski, I had to get into costume, too.

It was time for me to do my championship cannonball dive again.

"How's your butt?" asked Gloria.

"Will you *please* stop asking me about my butt?"

"Just doing my job, P.T." She checked something on her clipboard.

"My butt condition is listed on your clipboard?"

"Of course. Any job worth doing is worth doing well."

I slipped into my bathing suit, Hawaiian shirt, and flip-flops and headed out to the pool, where Cassie McGinty was meeting Porker D. Pigg, who definitely lived up to his name. He had to weigh at least four hundred pounds.

"He's big," said Cassie.

"He's a pig, man," said Aidan.

"I know," said Cassie. "But I was thinking more, you know, piglet."

"Nah. Those are just make-believe, like in *Winnie-the-Pooh*."

"Okay, everybody," hollered Dawg. "We're back at scene 701. Polly Pureheart meets Eric Von Wipple. Let's put the pig on the Jet Ski."

"Nope," said a man in bib overalls. "He ain't gonna be doin' that."

"What?"

"Porker cain't do that trick."

"Who are you?" asked the A.D.

"Dwight. I'm Porker's handler."

"Aiyyo, Dawg," said Aidan, "Dwight is the man who made Porker a YouTube superstar, so y'all need to get into *his* head space, man."

Dawg turned to the director. "Kurt? Problem with the stunt. Porker can't do the Jet Ski gag."

Kurt rubbed his face. "Okay. What can your pig do?"

"Well, sir, he can doggy-paddle."

"Can he fly off an underwater ramp?"

"Nope. He can doggy-paddle."

"Can he stand on a surfboard?" asked Cassie.

"Nuh-uh," said Dwight. "He can doggy-paddle."

"Let's just give it a try," I whispered to Cassie. "Please?"

"It might be funny," said Ms. Foxworth. "And we still might find Kevin. People everywhere are looking for him."

"But currently Porker is our only animal option," added Gloria.

"Okay, fine, whatever," Cassie said with a resigned sigh—one that sounded exactly like the kind Mom makes when she runs numbers through her calculator and realizes we're *this close* to being totally broke.

Aidan Tyler drifted off to grab a snack at the craft services table. I hoped it wasn't a double bacon cheeseburger.

Meanwhile, Dwight ushered Porker down the steps into the shallow end of the pool.

That took like five minutes. Maybe ten.

Aidan strolled back, munching a big bite of a crunchy apple.

"Yo, I appreciate y'all givin' this a try," he proclaimed. "I think Porker will prove to be a pretty genius choice."

"Um, you probably shouldn't be eating that right now," said Gloria.

"Whoa. Don't you start hating on me again, girl. . . ."

"*Squeeeee!*" squealed the pig. It snorted and sniffed with its rubbery snout.

Gloria tried again. "Like I said . . ."

Aidan chomped another chunk out of his apple.

Gloria threw up her arms. "Okay. Fine. Whatever."

"*Snort-snort-squee!*" roared the pig.

"Um, Dwight?" said Dawg. "We're about to roll camera and sound. Can we do something about the snorting and squealing?"

"Naw," said the pig handler. "That's just his way. Especially when he smells food. Did I forget to tell y'all not to bring no food nowheres too close to Porker?"

"*Squeeeeee! Snork-snork-snork.*"

The pig splashed and thrashed in the water. Dwight tried to hold on to his star, but remember, Porker weighed four hundred slick pounds. Dwight couldn't wrap his arms around the pig's ginormous waist. It was just too huge.

Cassie cracked up. "Okay. You were right, Aidan. This *is* hysterical."

And that was when the pig slipped out of Dwight's grip!

Cut to the Chase

Porker rushed out of the water.

Aidan took off running, clutching the apple he probably should've tossed.

The pig and the pig handler were in hot pursuit.

Go, Surf Piggy, you're ripping up the swimming pool!

Everybody else on the set howled with laughter.

"Roll all the cameras!" shouted Kurt. "Background actors—dance! This stuff is golden."

The sound guy bopped a button. Music blasted out of the speakers, giving us a great soundtrack for our improvised chase scene.

"And cut!" cried Kurt after Aidan and the snorting pig did three laps. The chase ended when Aidan finally tossed his half-eaten apple over his shoulder and Porker snagged it like a center fielder playing for the Poughkeepsie Pigs.

Cassie was rolling her eyes.

But I was feeling a ton better.

Aidan Tyler's goofy pig idea was so stupid it might actually work.

Go, Surf Piggy, you're running a surf boarding school!
You dance a jiggy, the girls go wiggy for Surf Piggy!

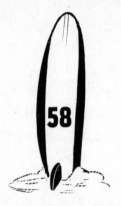

When Pigs Surf

I lost my big cannonball scene because Surf Pig couldn't ride a Jet Ski over a jump.

But I didn't care!

We were still filming the movie on location at the Wonderland. Our motel was going to be famous. We'd never have to sell out to Mr. Conch. Veronica could kiss her lazy river good-bye.

Of course, I was still worried about Kevin the Monkey. But somebody had to find him. Soon. Banana yellow codes are very effective.

The next morning, we were supposed to reshoot the big beach scene. Dwight, the pig wrangler, had actually figured out a way for Porker to stand on a surfboard, which would be strapped to the air tank of a very strong scuba diver who'd stay underwater and make it look like the pig was riding the waves.

Even though Aidan Tyler wasn't in the first part of the beach scene, he was on set.

"See? I told y'all this would work. Just like rock, paper, scissors. Surf Pig always beats Surf Monkey."

"Where's Cassie?" asked the director. "We're ready to roll."

"I haven't seen her," reported Gloria.

Kurt turned to his A.D. "Let's get Miss McGinty on set."

Dawg barked into his walkie-talkie. "Production? We need Miss McGinty on set."

A voice came back: "Um, she's not in her trailer."

"Try hair and makeup."

"Already did. She's not there."

"Have you checked with Ms. Foxworth?"

"This is Dawn," said a second voice over the radio. "I haven't seen her. This is so unprofessional. So unlike Cassie."

While we were standing around waiting for Cassie, Mr. Conch drifted down to our beach.

"Hey there, Petey. You folks have good sand. When we take over this patch of the beach, I'm thinking about sponsoring a sand-sculpture competition. You ever do one of those?"

"Not yet," I said. "But I'm going to."

"Sure. You can sign up. Anybody can. As long as they pay the entry fee."

"No, I mean I'm going to organize a sand-sculpture competition. . . ."

"Where?" he said with a laugh. "In your dreams?"

"Nope. Right here behind the Wonderland!"

"You mean the new wing of the Conch Reef Resort."

"Huh?"

"Talk to your mother, Petey." He pulled out his phone. Wiggle-waggled it at me. "Because she definitely wants to talk to me."

"No way."

Mr. Conch laughed. "Well, that's what she said in her message." He tapped the face of his phone. Mom's voice came out of the tinny speaker.

"Mr. Conch? This is Wanda Wilkie. We, uh, should probably talk. . . ."

"See you around, Petey. Don't forget—I always get what I want. Sometimes I just have to wait a little longer than usual." Still laughing, he ambled away.

Thirty minutes later, Dawg told all the dancers and actors to take an "early lunch." At ten a.m.

By eleven, everyone's concern had turned to worry.

By noon, it was pure panic.

"I can't shoot around the monkey *and* my leading

lady!" I heard Kurt say as he tugged at the hair on both sides of his head again.

"Aiyyo," Aidan said to his flunkies. "Maybe this whole movie should just be about me and the pig."

"True," said one of his minions.

"I don't need a fancy actress like Cassie McGinty seriousing everything up."

"You sure don't," said a different minion.

"It'd just be me and Porker. That's the movie I always wanted to do. Maybe my lady friend, Aisha, could be in it with me!"

"Awesome!" said his breath mint holder.

"Aisha and me? We'd have fo rizzle romantic sizzle. We'd hit the road. We'd see America. Porker D. Pigg could chase us around stuff. Now that's the kind of movie I'd pay to see me in! I'm so glad that funky monkey ran away!"

"Me too!" echoed all his hangers-on.

"Your pig movie would be even better if you shot it over here!" cried Veronica Conch, who must've been standing on a ladder again on her side of the fence. "And we'd stop serving our Brown Sugar Bacon Waffle Platter if it offended your costar."

My phone buzzed in my pocket. I had an incoming text.

From Cassie McGinty.

The Price of Fame

TELL MOM I'M SORRY.

IT'S ALL OVER THE INTERNET.

I HATE BEING FAMOUS!

Missing Movie Star

I texted her right back:

WHERE ARE YOU?

Cassie quickly replied:

IN HIDING.
4EVER!

My turn:

WHY?

Cassie sent me one more text and then went silent.

WATCH THE VIDEO.

IT'S ON YOUTUBE.

YOU'LL SEE.

I found Gloria in the lobby.

"What's up?" she said.

"Cassie just texted me."

"Where is she?"

"Hiding."

"Why?"

"Some kind of video on YouTube."

I fired up the app on my phone.

Mom was behind the front desk, talking on the phone.

"But we have you booked for three more weeks," I heard her say. She was curling her hair around a pencil. "You can't cancel all the rooms, Dawn. I'm sure Cassie will come back and everything will be fine. Video? What video?"

I motioned for Mom to join Gloria and me.

"Can I call you right back? Thank you." She hurried over.

"Did you really call Mr. Conch?" I asked.

"Yes, P.T. It seemed like a prudent move."

Great. We were back to the dented prunes.

"So what happened?" Mom asked. "Ms. Foxworth just told me that the studio chief, Lisa Norby Rook, is on a plane. She's coming here to shut down the production."

Your monkey ran away. Your leading lady ran away. And now this video on YouTube? We should call this movie <u>Beach Party Disasterville</u>!

"Apparently," said Gloria, "this video on YouTube has something to do with why Cassie has gone into hiding."

"She's in hiding?" said Mom.

"Yeah," I said, and touched the play button.

It was a shaky, amateur clip that had been edited into one long continuous loop. Cassie, costumed as Polly Pureheart, was standing near our pool. She kept repeating the same line over and over and over while the crew around her laughed: "AIDAN TYLER IS THE WORST ACTOR I'VE EVER WORKED WITH!" she screamed with authority.

"Oh, my," said Mom. "Mr. Tyler's not going to like that."

The clip played again and again. In the background, I could see my elbow.

Because I was the one who had directed Cassie's line reading.

There's No Motel Like Home

Gloria and I went to tell Ms. Foxworth that we'd heard from Cassie.

On the way, I let Gloria know how bummed I was.

"I really wanted to be famous. Not just for me— but for the Wonderland."

"You know, P.T., sometimes you remind me of my dad," said Gloria. "He really wants to be famous, too. To run with the big dogs on ESPN. To be seen on a bajillion TV screens at once. So we keep moving up and down the channels, hopping from one city to the next. But when you chase fame, you give up an awful lot."

"Like what?"

"Like never having a real home," said Gloria.

"What do you mean? You guys have a home. *This* is your home."

"No, P.T. This is a motel. A very nice motel, but it's still just a place where people sleep on their way to somewhere else."

She had a point, I figured.

But the Wonderland was my home. Mom and Grandpa's, too.

A home I had put in danger by insisting we make a movie. By not finding Kevin the Monkey when he ran away. By goofing around with Cassie McGinty, coaching her to say Aidan Tyler was a lousy actor louder and with more authority.

I guess Mom, Grandpa, and me were going to need a new motel of our own pretty soon.

Someplace to sleep on our way to wherever we might end up.

Missing Person Report

"Cassie's in hiding," I told Ms. Foxworth.

"But we don't know where," added Gloria.

"She's also turned off her phone," said Cassie's mom, sounding frustrated. "I can't reach her. And if she's not here when Lisa Norby Rook lands . . . with the monkey still missing . . . and the pig . . . and Aidan throwing a fit . . ."

She rubbed her eyes with one hand and waved us out of the room with the other.

"So, P.T., can I ask you something?" said Gloria as we walked through the motel grounds, which were still decorated for a movie nobody was making anymore.

"Sure," I told her. "What's up?"

"Just how deviously diabolical do you think Aidan Tyler is?"

"What do you mean?"

"What if he's the one who got rid of Kevin and Cassie?"

"Why would he do that?"

"So he could make the movie he really wanted to make. One with his girlfriend, Aisha, and Porker D. Pigg."

"Seriously?" I said. "You think he monkey-napped Kevin and then posted that video of Cassie?"

"It's a possibility. This morning he sounded so happy about Kevin and Cassie not being in the movie anymore. He has lots of pals in the paparazzi. He might've helped them shoot that shaky video. Aidan Tyler might be the one behind all this."

Fact: Gloria Ortega is one of the smartest people I know. So when she's thinking about something, I start thinking about it, too.

○ ○ ○

"I'm so sorry," I said when Mom, Grandpa, and I sat down to eat lunch together.

"We'll survive, P.T.," said Mom.

"We could start doing jewel thief tours again. And frog karaoke. That should get us some new guests."

Mom nodded. "It might. Or we could sell out to Mr. Conch. Move to a nice condo. Arizona could be fun."

Lunch was tomato soup with saltines. It's usually one of my favorites. Not that day.

"I don't want to sell the Wonderland to anybody," said Grandpa, slamming his soupspoon down on the table. "Except P.T. when he turns twenty-one. So we'll cut a few corners. Tighten our belts. We can even be prudent, Wanda. I'll go with the generic bologna instead of the Oscar Mayer. I'll cut out the pickle relish, too. But I'm not giving up my Cel-Ray! There is no such thing as generic celery soda."

We ate lunch mostly in silence.

Finally, Grandpa picked up his bowl and loudly slurped down the last drops of soup.

Mom dabbed at her lips with a paper napkin.

"If you guys will excuse me," she said, "I'm going to go sit with Dawn. She must be worried sick about Cassie."

Mom left.

The second she was gone, Grandpa cleared his throat.

Then he started glaring at me.

Bologna Bandits

"**Y**ou know, P.T.," said Grandpa, "you're my favorite grandson."

"Um, I'm your *only* grandson."

"True. And I think the world of you and all. But . . ."

He took a deep breath, left me hanging in suspense.

"But what?" I finally asked.

"Well, P.T., if I'm supposed to make do with sandwiches featuring store-brand luncheon meat, well, I really think *you* should be a little less wasteful."

"You mean like when I don't finish all the soda in the can because I start burping?"

"Nope, nope, nope. I'm talking about bologna, P.T. Oscar Mayer super-thick cut. The sixteen-ounce package."

"Oh-kay. And why, exactly, are you talking about that?"

"Because, P.T., on the very same day that Kevin the Monkey ran away, someone threw a half-full package—that's eight ounces of America's favorite fully cooked quality meat with no fillers—into the trash can in the parking lot. The one near the fence."

"And you think *I* tossed it out?" I said.

Grandpa shrugged. "You're young. Always in a rush. You don't fully appreciate the importance of high-quality pork products in resealable packaging."

"I'm sorry, Grandpa, but I'm not your bologna bandit."

"Oh, really?" Grandpa eyed me skeptically.

"Really. I'm not as crazy about bologna as you are. Actually, the only one who comes close is Kevin the—"

Yep.

I was having a lightbulb moment.

"Come on!" I said, standing up from the table. "Gloria was right!"

"Huh?" said Grandpa. "Where are we going?"

"The scene of the crime! But wait. First I need something."

I went to the fridge, found an open package of bologna, and peeled off a circular slice.

"Be careful with that, P.T.," said Grandpa.

"Don't worry. I won't drop it."

We dashed through the lobby and headed around back. I led Grandpa to the window outside J.J.'s first-floor room.

The dark circle was still on the concrete sill.

I held the bologna slice over the round stain.

"Go ahead," said Grandpa. "Put it down on the filthy, dirty ledge. It's not like I'm going to eat it after you've been running around, squeezing it with your fingers."

I placed the bologna on the darkened splotch.

It was a perfect fit.

Uninvited Guests

"You know," said Grandpa, "I read in a prank book once that bologna, or any food with nitrates in it, can stain the paint on a car."

"Looks like it will stain the paint on a window-sill pretty good, too!"

"Yo, motel boy? Old man?"

Aidan Tyler saw Grandpa and me standing in the hibiscus bushes.

I quickly stuffed the spongy slice of bologna into my pants pocket.

"When y'all are done peeping through that window, I need you to give my lady friend, Aisha, a hand with her bags. She's moving into Cee McG's room."

"Oh, we can't do that," said Grandpa. "Miss McGinty is still our registered guest."

"Naw, old man," said Aidan. "She can't be your guest, because she ain't here. So haul out her stuff, fluff up some towels, and move my girlfriend's gear on in."

Grandpa shook his head. "Nope, nope, nope. What you are suggesting is against all the time-honored traditions of the hospitality trade, Mr. Tyler. As far as the Wonderland Motel is concerned, Miss McGinty is still our guest."

"She's only been gone for like six hours," I reminded Aidan. "She'll be back."

"Well, if she do come back, she ain't working with me," said Aidan. "I saw that video, man. So did five million other people! What she said? It cut deep. Cee McG was hating on me."

"She was just goofing around," I said.

"Fine, man," said Aidan, puffing up his chest. "Y'all don't want the new costar of *Beach Party Surf Pig* staying with you, maybe the Conch Reef does. Maybe the Conch Reef would be a better location for my movie, too."

"Wait a second," I said. "*Your* movie? You can't change the location and the leading lady!"

"Aiyyo. I'm Aidan Tyler. I can do whatever I want to do, because right now I'm the only bona fide star still in the picture."

Aha! I thought. *Gloria was so totally right!*

Aidan Tyler was a sneaky genius. He wanted to

do a movie with his girlfriend and a pig, not Cassie and Kevin. He'd masterminded the whole thing.

All he'd needed to make the dominoes start tumbling was some vacuum-packed Oscar Mayer bologna.

And then he'd tossed the leftovers into the garbage can near the fence on his mad dash back to his room at the Conch Reef Resort!

Monkey Tail

I raced upstairs and knocked on Gloria's door.

"You were right!"

"Cool," she said. "About what, exactly?"

"Aidan Tyler. He kidnapped Kevin and set up Cassie."

"Can you prove it?"

"Maybe. If we can find where he's been hiding the monkey . . ."

"We could use that information to make him confess about planting the Cassie video, too!"

"Boom!"

Gloria and I fist-bumped on it.

"Quick question," said Gloria. "How exactly are we going to find Kevin?"

"Not sure. We could tail Aidan."

"Where is he?"

"Next door. Helping his girlfriend, Aisha, check into the Conch Reef."

I told Gloria about the circular bologna stain underneath the animal trainer's window.

"I think Aidan lured Kevin out of his room with the bologna."

Gloria nodded. "Because he undoubtedly heard from one of his flunkies how your grandfather lured Kevin out of that orange tree with processed meat."

"Exactly!"

Gloria glanced at her watch.

"The Conch Reef is still serving lunch. If this Aisha character just flew into town, she'll be hungry."

We hurried over to the Conch Reef. The restaurant smelled like deep-fried fish mixed with overcooked broccoli.

"Hello," said Veronica Conch, who was standing near the hostess stand. "What brings you two over here? Oh, wait. I know. You want to check out the new and improved location for *Beach Party Surf Pig,* starring the dynamic duo Aidan Tyler and Aisha, who doesn't have a last name, because she's like Adele and doesn't need one."

"Says who?" demanded Gloria.

"All the fan magazines. Aisha's hot and getting hotter."

"That's not what I meant," said Gloria. "Who says the movie's coming over here to shoot?"

"Aidan," said Veronica. "The Tyes. Don't believe me? Ask him yourself. He's inside at the buffet."

Veronica gestured grandly to her right.

Gloria and I hurried into the restaurant.

And saw Aidan Tyler throwing another one of his world-famous temper tantrums.

"I don't care if you don't have any!" he screamed at a waiter. "I need bananas!"

Ladies and gentlemen, we have our monkey-napper.

Spy Time

Gloria and I slumped down in a booth so Aidan couldn't see us.

We held menus in front of our faces, too.

A server came over. "What do you kids want?" She licked the tip of her pencil and poised it over a pad.

I dug a wad of crumpled cash out of my shorts. That slice of bologna? It was smooshed between my wrinkled one-dollar bills.

"What can we get for five bucks?" I asked, laying my money and luncheon meat on the table.

"Two Cokes," said the server, scooping up our menus with a dirty look. "And you can't bring in outside food. It's against the rules." She snagged my bologna, too.

Gloria and I nursed our watery soft drinks and

tried to stay hidden in our booth while Aidan waited for someone to bring him his bananas. When he finally left the restaurant with his Styrofoam to-go box, we gave him a thirty-second head start.

"He's going to lead us right to the monkey," whispered Gloria as we crept across the carpeted lobby.

"Then he'll have to confess to setting Cassie up," I said, "or we'll report him to the ASPCA. Maybe Aidan will even apologize. Cassie will forgive him and come back to the set. Everything will be the way it was."

"The Wonderland will be the most famous motel in America," added Gloria. "And you'll be the most famous butt in Hollywood."

"A cannonball dive isn't all about the butt, Gloria," I reminded her. "You need to grab your knees and tuck to assume the ball position. . . ."

We heard a bell ding.

Rounding a corner, we saw Aidan step into an elevator.

Gloria and I ran down the hall.

Watched the numbers climb.

"He has to be on the top floor," suggested Gloria, pressing the elevator call button. "The penthouse."

A second elevator dinged open its doors.

We hopped in and jabbed the PH button.

When we finally made it to the fourteenth floor,

a big beefy guy in gray slacks and a blue blazer, with a chest as wide as a cement mixer, was standing on the other side of the elevator doors.

"May I help youse two?" the security guard asked.

"Um, we're in the movie with Aidan Tyler," I said. "We were, uh, supposed to come up here and work on our scene with him."

The big guy just shook his head. Actually, he kind of wound it sideways a few times. It's hard to *shake* your head when your neck is the size of a fire hydrant.

"Not today. This floor is off-limits. Beat it, kids."

I tried to say something. "But—"

"What part of 'beat it' didn't you understand?"

The elevator doors slid shut.

I might've been imagining things as Gloria and I rode back down to the lobby, but just as we left the top floor, somewhere, off in the distance, I could've sworn I heard a monkey screech!

Taking the Tour

We ran back to the Wonderland and enlisted Grandpa's help.

"We need an adult," I told him.

"And I'm the best you could do? Fine. What's the caper?"

"We think Aidan Tyler has Kevin the Monkey locked up in a room next door," explained Gloria. "Somewhere on the top floor."

"He took a bunch of bananas up there," I added. "And I'm not one hundred percent certain, but when we were riding down in the elevator, I think I heard a monkey screech."

"I thought I heard that, too!" said Gloria.

Grandpa rubbed his hands together. "Okay. Here's what we do. We go next door and sell out!"

"Wha-hut?" said Gloria.

Grandpa winked. "It's what we call a clever ruse."

"Why?" I asked.

"Because it'll be an ingenious trick. You kids need to start learning better vocabulary words at that middle school you're going to!"

The three of us trooped over to the Conch Reef.

"Is Eddie here?" Grandpa asked the manager behind the front desk.

"You mean Mr. Conch?" sniffed the manager. He had a very thin mustache and a very snooty 'tude.

"Yeah," said Grandpa. "I'm Walt Wilkie from next door. Eddie wants to buy us out. At first, I said no. Now? Maybe I'm changing my mind."

"I see," purred the manager. "Well, Mr. Conch isn't here at the moment. Perhaps I can be of assistance?"

"Fine by me, Bryce," said Grandpa, reading the man's badge.

(That's one of the great things about working in the hospitality trade: everybody wears a name tag.)

"Like I said, I'm interested in giving your boss what he wants. But to be honest, I've been running the Wonderland since the 1970s. It'll be hard for me to pass her on to somebody new."

Grandpa cleverly left out the part where Mr. Conch bulldozes our motel into the dust.

"So," he said, "before I sell, I need to know you guys are as good as you seem."

"Oh, we are, sir. Even better, sir. Trust me, sir."

"Can you prove it?"

"Most definitely. I can show you our ranking on TripAdvisor, Yelp . . ."

"Nope, nope, nope. I'm not interested in all that Internet mumbo jumbo. I want a tour."

"I see. And when would be a convenient time?" Bryce clicked his pen. Repeatedly.

"How about now?" asked Grandpa. "Does now work?"

"But of course." Bryce bopped a bell. Another worker in a shrimp-pink tunic scampered behind the desk.

"Yes, Bryce?"

"Take over the front, Abigail. I need to lead a tour. For Mr. Conch."

"Yes, sir. Of course, sir."

Bryce swept out from behind the front desk, flashing us his card key. It was attached to a pull cable that came out of a silver spool clipped to his belt.

"This card opens each and every door on the property," he proudly announced. "Shall we start at the pool?"

"If it's okay with you, Bryce," said Grandpa, "let's start at the top. I've always wanted to check out your world-class penthouse views."

"Of course," said Bryce. "Unfortunately, all of

the suites on the fourteenth floor are currently occupied. Movie stars and their entourages . . ."

"Bryce," said Grandpa, "let me ask you a question."

"Certainly, sir."

"If the president of the United States unexpectedly checked in right now, could you find him a penthouse suite?"

"Why, of course, sir. Immediately."

"Well, buddy, I got news for you. The president isn't coming to Florida today. So show us the room you were going to give him."

And just like that, we were on our way, back up to the top floor.

Going Bananas

When the elevator doors slid open on the top floor, the large guard was blocking the way again.

"This floor is closed," he grunted.

"It's okay," said the snooty manager. "I'm Bryce Byrd. I report directly to Mr. Conch."

"He's giving us a tour," added Grandpa. "And so far, all I'm seeing is you."

Bryce flicked his wrist. "Step aside, sir, if you please."

The security goon moved out of our way.

We bustled off the elevator.

"Now, obviously, I can't take you into any occupied rooms," said Bryce.

"We could at least ask to take a peek," said Grandpa. "Where's the harm in asking?"

While Grandpa and the hotel manager bickered,

Gloria and I slipped down the hall toward the service elevator.

It glided open.

A bellhop pushing a cart came out.

A cart loaded down with banana crates!

We followed the rumbling cargo down the hall. The air behind it smelled like those jumbo bags of spongy circus peanut candies they sell at the grocery store. The bellhop came to a stop in front of a locked door near the fire exit at the far end of the hall.

He was about to unlock it when that fire exit door swung open.

"P. T. Wilkie?" said an annoyingly familiar voice. "What're you two doing up here?"

Veronica Conch.

Opening Doors

"**D**on't you dare open that door!" Veronica snapped at the bellhop.

"Yes, ma'am."

"Mr. Byrd?" she called down the hall. Bryce and Grandpa were still arguing about what we'd be allowed to see.

"Miss Conch," sputtered Bryce, prancing up the carpet like an eager reindeer. "I can explain. . . ."

"What's in that room?" I asked, nodding toward the door with the banana cart parked in front of it.

"None of your beeswax," said Veronica. She turned on her sparkly red sneakers to face the manager. "No unauthorized guests are allowed on these floors, Mr. Byrd. Not while *Beach Party Surf Pig* is in production."

"We were just taking the tour," said Grandpa.

"What tour?" demanded Veronica.

"The one I need to take before I sell my motel to your father."

"Oh. You're finally interested in making a deal with Daddy?"

"Maybe. If everything checks out."

Veronica beamed. "It's like Daddy says. At Conch High-Quality Resorts, you always get what you want because he always gets what he wants!"

"Right," I said. "I've seen his bumper sticker. But why can't we see what's inside that room?"

"There isn't a Do Not Disturb sign hanging on the doorknob," said Grandpa. "Open it up, Bryce."

"No!" said Veronica. "It might prove . . . embarrassing."

Because that's where Aidan Tyler is keeping Kevin the Monkey! I thought. *And Veronica Conch is helping him!*

"We can show you a room on the tenth floor," suggested Veronica.

"Oh, yes," said Bryce. "The tenth floor is very luxurious. VIP suites for our platinum preferred medallion members."

Grandpa shook his head.

"Nope, nope, nope. I want to see a room up here. This one will do just fine."

"No way, Mr. Wilkie," said Veronica.

"Young lady," said Grandpa, sounding sterner

than I'd ever heard him sound before, "either you open that door right now or I'm calling your father and telling him exactly why our deal is never, ever going to happen. I will also tell him that it's all your fault!"

Veronica looked at Grandpa.

He didn't blink.

Veronica did.

Left in the Dark

"**W**hatever," said Veronica before sticking out her tongue and blowing a raspberry. "I don't care. Open the stupid door, Bryce."

The hotel manager swiped his card key and swung open the door.

The room was pitch-dark.

Until he flicked a switch.

Then we saw that the "room" was actually a housekeepers' supply closet, crammed full of tiny shampoo bottles, toilet paper rolls, miniature mouthwashes, and stacks of folded towels.

There was also a life-size cardboard cutout of Aidan Tyler. Plus Aidan Tyler posters, lunch boxes, hats, dolls . . . and dental floss. Seriously. Veronica Conch had a carton of Aidan Tyler dental floss dispensers.

"I told you this would be totally embarrassing," said Veronica.

"You were correct," said Gloria. "Is that an Aidan Tyler piñata?"

"Yuh-huh. It's filled with purple jelly beans. His favorite color and flavor. Aidan doesn't know what a huge fan I am! That's why I can't stand your over-rated friend Cassie McGinty trashing him in that YouTube video."

"She was just horsing around," I said. "That clip was taken out of context."

"No," said Veronica. "She said that mean stuff about Aidan. And then you, P. T. Wilkie, you made her say it again. Louder and with more authority!"

"What's with all the bananas?" asked Grandpa.

"We just started hauling them up here," explained the bellhop. "Mr. Tyler insisted that we never run out of bananas again."

"Aha!" I said. "This proves it!"

"Proves what?" said Veronica.

"That Aisha is on one whacked-out diet," said someone behind us.

Aidan Tyler.

Banana Appeal

"**A**isha won't eat nothing but bananas," said Aidan, grabbing a bunch out of a box. "Some California nutrition guru put her on the all-banana diet. Aiyyo—you should smell her burps."

"You really expect us to believe that all these bananas are for your girlfriend?" I said.

"Yeah," said Aidan with a shrug. "Why else?"

"How about for Kevin the Monkey?" said Gloria.

"Yo—did he come back? Because me and Aisha still want to make our movie with Porker D. Pigg. Monkey had his shot, man. Monkey blew it."

A voice came from up the hall: "Aidan? Where are my bananas? I need a snack!"

"Yo, I'm workin' on it, baby."

Shaking his head, Aidan started up the hall, cradling his fruit.

"Girl's gonna drive me cray-cray," he muttered.

"Can we check out your rooms?" I blurted out.

Aidan shrugged. "I don't care. Just don't slip on all the banana peels, man."

And just like that, we were in his room and then Aisha's and then the six other rooms the members of his entourage were using.

Two of them stank like rotten bananas. Aidan's and Aisha's.

The fifth room, PH-13, where some of Aidan's flunkies were bunking, stank like something worse.

"It's coming from the vent in the bathroom," said Aidan's hairdresser, fanning his hand under his nose. "Whoever is in the room downstairs needs to eat a few less bean burritos."

"For your information, sir," said Veronica, "room 1313 is currently vacant. The odors are most likely coming up from the kitchen."

"Really?" said the hairdresser. "What are you guys serving today? Fart stew?"

It needs more rotten eggs and swamp gas.

"If we are serving fart stew," said snarky Veronica, "I'll be sure to send you up a big bowl, buster!"

"I'll have a word with maintenance," said Bryce, "see what we can do about the unpleasant odors."

"No need, Mr. Byrd," said Veronica. "I will take care of it myself."

"Yo, you better," said Aidan, who was hanging with us on our mini-tour so he wouldn't have to watch Aisha mash more bananas in a blender. "'Cause if this nasty stank isn't out of this room by the time Lisa Norby Rook gets here from Hollywood, ain't no way me and Aisha are filming *Beach Party Surf Pig* here at the Conch Reef Resort. We'll be taking our movie up the beach to the Don CeSar!"

Take Two, Again

"Sorry, kiddos," said Grandpa as we hiked back to the Wonderland.

We'd checked out all the occupied rooms on the penthouse floor. We'd even nosed around in a couple of the empty ones. There was no sign of Kevin the Monkey. All those bananas? They really were for Aisha. And yes, she burped while we were in her room. It was worse than Grandpa's Cel-Ray gas attacks.

"Maybe Kevin just ran away," said Gloria. "Maybe he didn't want to be in the movies anymore."

"What?" I said. "Give up show business? Are you crazy? He's famous. No way would he give that up for a boring life being a nobody swinging in a tree."

Gloria looked at me and shook her head.

"You really have a thing about being famous, don't you, P.T.?"

"I guess. . . ."

"Not me," said Grandpa. "Being famous is how you end up eating nothing but bananas all day like that poor Aisha girl. I like some nice whitefish on crackers every now and then. Or matzo ball soup. Maybe a pastrami on rye . . ."

Grandpa drifted back to his workshop to fix himself a sandwich.

Gloria and I flopped down in a pair of poolside lounge chairs. Since the movie was more or less on hold without Cassie, most of the crew had headed to Tampa to ride the rides at Busch Gardens. Down on the beach, people were having fun, splashing in the surf, building sand castles. A couple of prop planes puttered along, dragging banners advertising the all-you-can-eat buffet at the Conch Reef Resort.

But the Wonderland felt empty. Deserted.

"I guess this is how it will be for a while," said Gloria. "Nobody here but you, me, my dad, and your mom."

"Because I told Mom to kick everybody else out," I reminded her. "Well, at least we'll be close to all the lights, cameras, and action over at the Conch Reef Resort, if Veronica can clear out the fart gas. I can't believe our movie is moving over there."

"I can't believe Veronica Conch. Why do all of her shoes have sparkles and spangles on them?"

"Because it's glitzy," I said. "She loves pizzazz and glamour and stars and glitter—"

I stopped. Stood up. Pointed at the back wall of our motel.

"What?" said Gloria, sounding worried.

"The sparkles. In the shrubbery."

"Oh-kay. Are you seeing some kind of magical unicorn?"

"No. Under the window. Where I found the bologna stain. I remember something glinting in the sand beneath the bushes. I thought it was just crushed seashells. . . ."

"Huh?"

"I used to collect 'em. The shiny kind. Now Grandpa mashes them up to sprinkle in the flower beds because they shimmer. Tells kids it's fairy dust. Come on."

We went back to the bush below the window of the animal trainer's room.

I dropped to my knees. So did Gloria.

I found a couple of sparkly objects that definitely weren't crushed sea-shells. For one thing, they were plastic, with circular holes cut in their centers. For another, they were bright red.

Seashells? I think not.

Sequins. From Veronica's shoes. I held three of them on my finger.

Ruby Slipper Slipup

"Looks like Veronica was wearing her 'ruby slippers' when she helped Kevin the Monkey climb out the window to fetch his bologna," I said.

"Wait a second," said Gloria. "Now you think Veronica Conch, not Aidan Tyler, kidnapped Kevin?"

"Yep. And she lost a few sequins in the sand."

"What was her motive?"

"Simple. She *looooves* glitz and glamour. And Aidan Tyler. Plus, she hates me."

"What?"

"Remember? She told us that her father says nice things about me and our moneymaking schemes." I snapped my fingers. "Wait a second. That wasn't in the YouTube video."

"Huh?" said Gloria, because I wasn't making much sense.

"That thing she said. About me coaching Cassie to say Aidan was a lousy actor louder and with more authority. It wasn't in the clip."

Now I whacked my forehead.

"Duh! *She* filmed it! I remember seeing her on the other side of the fence. Veronica's the one who hijacked our monkey and tried to sabotage our movie."

It was all making sense.

"She did it to show her 'daddy' that she could be as clever as me."

"Impossible," said Gloria, because she's my best bud. "No one could be *that* clever."

"Thanks. But if she forced us to sell our motel by ruining our movie and then she made the Conch Reef Resort famous by stealing that movie, come on—even Mr. Conch would have to be impressed with a double whammy like that. Plus, if Aidan and Aisha shoot *Beach Party Surf Pig* at the Conch Reef Resort, Veronica might get to be a background extra. Maybe in one big scene, she'd do a cannonball dive into the swimming pool. She'd become famous. I bet she'd love that."

"Hmmm," said Gloria. "Sounds familiar."

"I know. It sounds like me. The *old* me."

"Really? And when did the old you become the new one?"

"About two minutes ago. When I realized how

much trouble my family's going to be in if the Wonderland stays as empty as it is right now. And don't forget, Veronica Conch was right there behind the Sea Spray Motel when Grandpa coaxed Kevin out of the orange tree with the bologna!"

Gloria started piecing it all together. "First she thinks about stealing our Pirate Chest Treasure Quest idea. Then she gets ambitious. Decides to totally ruin the film shoot. She sics that yappy dog on Kevin. When that doesn't shut down production, she kidnaps Kevin the Monkey and publicly embarrasses Cassie McGinty, forcing her into hiding, taking her out of the picture. That means Aidan Tyler, even though he's a horrible actor, can make all sorts of demands. He can cast his girlfriend as the new female lead. And, most importantly, he can insist that the production company change locations to the Conch Reef Resort, where he's already in love with the breakfast buffet!"

"Exactly!" I said.

"Way to go, P.T.! Now we just have to figure out where Veronica is hiding Kevin the Monkey."

"Easy," I said. "Room 1313."

Lucky Thirteen

"**R**oom 1313?" said Gloria, eyeing me skeptically. "And how did you come up with that number?"

"Simple deduction. Remember PH-13?"

Gloria waved her hand under her nose. "How could I forget it?"

"Well, PH-13 is right above 1313. If Kevin's been locked up in that room for a couple days, it's got to be pretty rank. I don't think monkeys are potty-trained."

We both looked at the Conch Reef Resort, on the other side of the fence.

"You know," I said, "a lot of hotels, even the super-tall ones, don't have a thirteenth floor. It's considered bad luck."

"So what comes between the twelfth and fourteenth floors?"

"Nothing," I told her. "They just skip it."

"So," said Gloria, "how do we prove all of this? Should we call the police?"

I stared at the head and shoulders of that giant pirate statue Veronica had erected near the Conch Reef's swimming pool.

"We're not calling anybody," I said.

"And why not?"

"Because Veronica would just stall them while she shifted Kevin to a different room."

"So what do we do?"

"What I do best: tell a story—a ghost story!"

I went into Grandpa's workshop and grabbed his old megaphone.

"Where are you going with that, P.T.?" asked Grandpa.

"Next door. I'm picking up your clever ruse."

"Oooh. Tell me more."

"I'll pretend that since we're thinking about selling out to the Conch Reef Resort, we need to see if they attract the same kind of customers we do—tourists who enjoy a good spiel and an offbeat attraction."

"I see," said Grandpa patiently. "But what are we really doing?"

Gloria told him: "Rescuing Kevin the Monkey from room 1313!"

The Ghost on the
Thirteenth Floor

Grandpa grabbed the last of his bologna, and the three of us headed next door.

"Ladies and gentlemen, boys and girls, gather round to hear the bone-chilling tale of Pirate Pete, the ghost of the thirteenth floor!"

I was in full carnival barker mode, near the pool behind the Conch Reef Resort. Fortunately, Veronica was busy inside—hostess duty at the restaurant. Mr. Conch was off making another deal.

"Oh, my," said Bryce, the manager, who scuttled out of the hotel to see what all the fuss was about. "What's going on back here?"

"Final test of our compatibility, Bryce," Grandpa told him confidentially. "My grandson is trying out *his* shtick with *your* guests."

"P.T. is quite an entertainer," said Gloria. "In fact, his storytelling prowess has made him one of the Wonderland Motel's most valuable assets, centers of excellence, and revenue streams. He is what we call a cash cow."

"Oh. I see," said Bryce, sounding impressed, the way people usually do when Gloria starts spouting business buzzwords. "He *has* attracted quite a crowd."

"And," whispered Grandpa, "when he's done, you can sell all these folks souvenirs."

"With P. T. Wilkie on board," added Gloria, "the Conch Reef Resort can leapfrog its competition and revive its gift shop market share at the granular level."

Bryce just nodded.

I kept spinning my yarn.

"It took thirteen cannonballs fired from thirteen different ships to end Pirate Pete's thirteenth adventure on the high seas. He fell overboard. His faithful monkey, Screech, whom Pete had befriended during one of his raids along the Barbary Coast, dove into the ocean and, with the help of a friendly dolphin, dragged that poor dead pirate's body to shore. Then the monkey scooped up the sand, right over there"—I pointed toward the main hotel building— "and buried his pirate master. Exhausted from all that digging, wishing he'd had a shovel instead of just monkey paws, Screech fell into the same grave and died on top of his pirate master, becoming one more monkey on a dead man's chest. And that's why, to this very day, if you ride the hotel elevators up to the thirteenth floor, you will hear Pirate Pete's anguished moans and Screech the monkey's terrified shrieks."

"You're making this junk up!" said a kid in the crowd.

I smiled slyly and put on my "talk like a pirate" voice.

"Am I, laddie? Aaaar. Room 1313, that's where they both be. But who here is brave enough amongst ye to give me the key?"

"I will!" shouted Bryce, who I think was more into my ghost story than he should've been for a guy his age.

"And who," I said to the crowd, "is brave enough to join us on our terrifying quest into the triskaidekaphobia zone?"

"Me!" shouted everybody.

"And afterward," asked a different kid, "can we buy, like, a Screech the monkey stuffed animal in your gift shop or a bag of chocolate pirate coins?"

I saw Gloria smile at Bryce. "See what I mean? Cash. Cow."

The Guest in Room 1313

Two dozen tourists followed me, Gloria, Grandpa, and Bryce (the man with the magical master key) into the hotel lobby.

Everybody was extremely excited as we crammed into both elevators for the ride up to the "Haunted Thirteenth Floor"!

When we stepped off on thirteen, everybody smelled monkey poop.

"P.U.," said a little girl, wrinkling up her nose as we slowly made our way down the hall. "What's that smell?"

"Ectoplasm," I said, because I've seen the movie *Ghostbusters* a million times. "It always smells like that when ghosts are near. Just don't let them slime you."

The thirteenth floor was eerily empty. No

housekeeping carts were parked in the corridor. No room service trays were sitting on the floor outside doors.

As we passed room 1311, I heard a monkey screech.

Kevin was calling to us from 1313.

"How'd you do that monkey screech, P.T.?" Bryce whispered. "Are you a professional ventriloquist, too?"

"A good performer never reveals his secrets," I whispered back. "Now then, Bryce," I said aloud, "if you will kindly open the door, it's time for everybody to meet Screech!"

"This is so cool!" said a kid.

"I want to buy *two* monkeys at the gift shop!" said another.

"This is just like the Haunted Mansion at Disney World," said a dad.

"Yes," I said, "but without the long drive or the longer lines!"

Bryce excitedly fumbled with his card key. He was starting to see the Haunted Thirteenth Floor as the gold mine Gloria told him it could be.

But then the elevator pinged open behind us.

"What do you people think you're doing up here?" Veronica Conch marched down the hallway. "Step away from that door."

"That's where the pirate's ghost monkey is!"

said a six-year-old, holding her nose. "Screech. He's stinky."

"Who wants to meet the stinky ghost monkey?" I asked.

"We do, we do!" said everybody.

Bryce extended his card key on its cable.

"Don't you dare!" shrieked Veronica.

"We want the monkey," the kids started chanting. "We want the monkey!"

Behind the locked door, Kevin started chittering and chattering.

Shocked (and looking like he'd just heard a ghost), Bryce dropped his card key. It dangled on its taut cord down near his knee.

I grabbed it—and swiped it across the lock pad before Veronica could stop me.

I pulled open the door and ducked.

My smartest move all day.

Because when that door flung open, a very agitated monkey was standing on the other side.

Kevin was not happy.

So he did what he'd done the last time he was mad.

He hurled a poop ball.

It hit Veronica Conch—right in the face.

Monkeying Around
with Gators

Grandpa gave Kevin a slice of bologna and the monkey hopped up on his shoulder.

"Are you Pirate Pete?" asked the six-year-old girl, who was still holding her nose.

"Narrgh," said Grandpa, because that's how pirates say no.

Then he turned to Veronica.

"The deal is off. Call your father. Tell him what you did. No way will I ever sell my property to a known monkey-napper!"

Veronica didn't say a word. She was too busy sobbing and wiping monkey poop off her face.

We took Kevin back to the Wonderland and called J.J., who was out on patrol with the ASPCA, searching for her primate friend. She was thrilled to hear the news.

With Kevin safely back in his room, I begged Grandpa to drive Gloria and me to Smugglers Cove.

Because I had a hunch Cassie McGinty might be there.

"Really?" he said. "Why?"

I pointed at one of our concrete benches. It's molded to look like an alligator.

"I'm guessing she wanted to meet Ugly Gus. Sooner or later, anyone who's ever been a kid does."

I was right.

But it took us like fifteen minutes to find her. I guess when you're a movie star, you learn a lot about makeup and disguises.

"I wanted to play Putt-Putt and feed the alligators," she told me. "I just wanted to be a normal kid for a couple hours."

"I don't blame you," I said.

"Plus," she reminded me, "I had a free pass."

"Just don't go swimming with the alligators, like P.T. theoretically did," said Gloria with an eye roll.

"I'm sorry I ruined the movie," said Cassie.

"You didn't ruin it," I said. "You just gave everybody a day off. But now Kevin's back, you're back . . ."

"But Aidan won't be back. He'll never forgive me for saying that mean stuff about him on YouTube."

And that gave me an idea.

For a new YouTube video.

I told it to Cassie. "We just have to make up a new story to make everybody forget that old one. When we spin the story this way, this is just something you like to randomly scream. It'll be funny. Everybody will get that it was just a joke."

Cassie smiled. "Thank you, P.T."

She pulled off her glasses, wig, and rubber nose. Gloria held up her phone to shoot the video.

And then Academy Award–winning actress Cassie McGinty screamed at the gators swirling around in the feeding lagoon: "GUS THE ALLIGATOR IS THE WORST ACTOR I'VE EVER WORKED WITH!"

It was pretty hysterical, if I do say so myself.

Within minutes, it had a million more thumbs-ups than the first video with her screaming about Aidan Tyler.

"Tomorrow," I told Cassie, "we need to shoot a third video. You can scream at a pelican."

YOU COULDN'T GET A PART IN <u>PETER PAN</u>!

Hooray for Hollywood

About an hour later, Lisa Norby Rook, the studio chief at Dreamscope Pictures, arrived at the Wonderland.

A quick meeting was convened poolside with Cassie and her mom. I pretended to be skimming leaves out of the pool with a net on a pole so I could eavesdrop on their conversation.

"I looked at the dailies on the plane ride," said Ms. Norby Rook.

"They're awful," said Cassie. "Right?"

"Not entirely. In fact, you're great. The music's great. But . . ."

"Aiyyo." Aidan Tyler bopped over. Aisha wasn't with him. "Cassie, you're looking fly."

"Fly?" said Cassie with a chuckle. "What does that even mean, Aidan?"

"That, um, you look nice? And I've totally forgiven you for that YouTube dealio. I didn't know you screamed that at alligators and stuff, too."

"Aidan," said Ms. Norby Rook, "we need to talk."

"Yes, ma'am."

The Tyes had completely dropped his attitude and swagger. I guess being face to face with the head of a major movie studio will do that to a guy. Especially when that head is sort of frowning like she has acid indigestion.

"I watched the footage of the scenes you folks shot," said Ms. Norby Rook. "I spotted some major . . . issues."

"The pig?" said Aidan. "If that's a problem for you, no worries. We can, like, definitely go back to the monkey, now that he's safe and all."

"Actually, Aidan, this is very difficult for me to say, but, well . . ."

"You're a terrible actor!" Kurt had just arrived on the scene. "The worst I ever worked with! You're going to ruin my reputation! You're a career wrecker!"

"Well, you're a hack!" Aidan shouted back. "You couldn't direct your way out of a paper bag!"

"I know," said the director, "because I'd need the bag to barf in while you stumbled through your lines four thousand times without getting a single one right."

It went on like that for maybe ten minutes.

Long story short, Aidan Tyler threatened to quit.

To make the story even shorter, Lisa Norby Rook said, "Okay, Aidan, if that's what you need to do. It definitely works for me. We'll tear up your contract."

Cassie's mom added, "Now you can go do that music tour."

Kurt told Aidan, "Take that stupid pig with you."

"Pigs are the seventh-smartest animals on the planet, man," said Aidan.

Then he stormed next door to the Conch Reef to pack up his things.

Everybody else sighed, sat down, and stayed quiet.

Finally, Cassie said the words I was afraid somebody had to say.

"So I guess that's a wrap. We pull the plug on *Beach Party Surf Monkey* and head home?"

Her mom and Ms. Norby Rook both nodded.

"We can't make the movie without a male lead," said Kurt. "I mean, you're great, Cassie. Kevin the Monkey's hysterical. But without someone to play Eric Von Wipple . . ."

And that was when I had my best blockbuster brainstorm ever!

Motel Movie Magic

You guessed it!

I pitched my buddy Pinky Nelligan for the lead role.

"You heard him sing, Kurt," I said to the director. "You saw him dance. He's incredible!"

"He's also pretty cute," added Cassie.

Then Gloria backed us up with all sorts of statistics about "target market demographics" and Pinky "hitting the sweet spot between cute and cool."

Then she dazzled them with some more gobbledy-gook about how pairing Pinky and Cassie could potentially turn *Beach Party Surf Monkey* into "a four-quadrant movie, appealing to all four slices of the demographic pie: males and females; under- and over-twenty-fives." She added, "It could be a tentpole franchise, guys."

Heads started nodding.

"He's the kid with the red hair and freckles?" said Ms. Norby Rook. "In the surfboard dance sequence?"

"Correct," said Cassie's mom. "Sings like an angel."

"Kid's a natural," added Kurt.

"I liked that footage," said Ms. Norby Rook. "Mostly because Aidan wasn't in it . . ."

"And think of the publicity spin this will give the flick," I said, trying my best to sound Hollywood-ish. "Unknown talent discovered at the Wonderland Motel. A star is born!"

And that's exactly what happened.

We finished filming three weeks later.

My family's incredibly cool motel was featured in just about every shot, except, of course, the ones out in the ocean.

Pinky was terrific as the preppy Eric Von Wipple. When he and Polly Pureheart finally kissed, everybody on the set oohed and aahed.

Well, everybody except me. I don't really go for the mushy stuff.

Gloria, with her business smarts, helped Cassie's mom keep the film under budget, which, we found out, is considered a major miracle in Hollywood. I think Lisa Norby Rook is going to offer Gloria a job the second she graduates college.

Gloria was even able to wrangle her dad the first exclusive red-carpet interview with Cassie and Pinky at the movie's gala Florida premiere.

You two left it all on the screen today. You definitely brought your A game, because you came to play. You knew what had to be done and you went out there and did it.

Gloria and I agreed: it's a good thing that an ESPN sportscaster job is her dad's dream. He wouldn't do so well on *Access Hollywood*.

Pinky didn't come back to Ponce de León Middle School right away. He was too busy out in LA, making more movies. Mark my word, in two years Pinky Nelligan will be bigger than Aidan Tyler. He'll be nicer, too.

Me?

Well, my cannonball dive didn't make the final cut. But my elbow did.

And that was fine by me.

Because I realized some things: If I became super famous, I might never be able to go to Crabby Bill's or Smugglers Cove without wearing a disguise, like Cassie had to. I'd have to live in Hollywood, and I like it here in Florida. Plus, I'd miss coming up with new ideas and new attractions, not to mention the stories that go along with them.

By the way, I am seriously considering doing that sand-sculpture competition thing—before the Conch Reef Resort next door beats us to it. I can see it now! People from all over will come to the Wonderland's famous beach. I'm also going to convince Mom that we need to open a restaurant. Maybe an outdoor grill near the pool, with a thatched palm roof and *Surf Monkey* decorations! It'll be huge. To keep Grandpa happy, we'll make sure bologna in some shape or form is always on the menu.

Plus, Mom needs my help behind the front desk. You wouldn't believe how many reservations have been pouring in since the movie premiered. Everybody all over the world wants to stay in the *Beach Party Surf Monkey* motel. We're hearing from people from Europe and South America and China and, of course, Canada. It gets cold in Canada. Helen

Nelson, our loyal long-term lodger from Toronto? She's coming back at her regular time next winter!

So anyway, Dad, wherever you are, I hope you catch *Beach Party Surf Monkey,* coming soon to a theater near you. If you do, you'll see our motel, maybe my elbow, and everything you've been missing all these years.

Because there is one thing we're famous for here at the Wonderland: having a wonderful time!

Don't miss the next
outrageously ridiculous
P. T. Wilkie tale!

WELCOME TO
WonderLand
Banana Shack Shake-Up

Coming in 2018!

P. T. Wilkie's

Outrageously
Ridiculous
and
Occasionally
Useful
Stuff

P.T. and Gloria's Unofficial Movie Credit Survival Guide

Grip: If you think handling cameras is a walk in the park, you'd better get a grip! Grips are responsible for building and maintaining the equipment that supports cameras. Grips also move and set up the equipment, making them instrumental to the filming process.

Key Grip: Key grips play the key role of supervising teams of grips.

Dolly Grip: Dolly grips move camera cranes and dollies, which are the wheeled platforms that carry the cameras and the camera operators around. Basically just remember this equation: camera + hoverboard = dolly grip.

Gaffer: Gaffers light up every room they walk into—literally! A gaffer is the head of the electrical department for a film production.

Child Wrangler: Child actors are anything but child's play! They need to be cared for, coached, entertained, and kept quiet between scenes. Child wranglers provide these services.

Python Wrangler: Lucky for them, python wranglers don't deal with any actual snakes! They are sound technicians who perform many tasks in the sound department, often pulling cables.

Foley Artist: In movies, fights are staged, so where do those *WHAM! KAPOW! SMASH!* sounds come from? The Foley artist! Foley artists add necessary sound effects to the movie so that it sounds realistic.

Best Boy: Back in the day, when the head of the grip or electrical department needed extra help, they would go to the other department and say, "Lend me your best boy." Nowadays this term just means the second-in-command to the gaffer or the key grip. The best boy can, of course, be a girl (although the title remains the same).

Fixer: If the crew is in a fix when it comes to permits, customs, location, talent, equipment, or transportation for filmmakers who want to film abroad, the fixers are there to fix the problem! Basically, they provide logistical support if (when) there are any problems with getting filming under way.

Craft Service: Think the cheese instead of arts and crafts. Craft service provides food for the cast and crew. They also are responsible for cleaning the set.

P. T. and Gloria's
Fact or Fiction Quiz:
Movie Edition!

(Circle your answer and find out if you're correct at ChrisGrabenstein.com.)

1. A chimp named Bonzo and former president Ronald Reagan starred in a movie called *Bedtime for Bonzo* in 1951.

FACT or FICTION

2. In *Teen Beach Movie,* Mack and Brady get sucked into the musical *Wet Side Story,* which is based on a real-life musical called *South Side Story.*

FACT or FICTION

3. *Marley & Me, Edward Scissorhands,* and *The Avengers* were filmed in Florida.

FACT or FICTION

4. The first movie theater in the United States was called the Nickelodeon. It only cost a dime to see a movie there, and it opened in 1905.

FACT or FICTION

5. Johnny Depp starred in the most expensive movie ever made.

FACT or FICTION

6. After years of only silent films, movies with sound were called speakies.
FACT or FICTION

7. Originally, movie theater operators didn't want to serve popcorn; they were worried that the snack would get all over the floor and make the theaters dirty.
FACT or FICTION

8. Chris Grabenstein's dog, Fred, appeared on Broadway in *Hamilton*.
FACT or FICTION

9. The longest movie ever made is 720 hours (thirty days) long.
FACT or FICTION

10. A killer whale named Keiko earned $36 million for starring in a movie called *Free Billy*.
FACT or FICTION

11. Walt Disney holds the record for winning the most Oscars for an individual.
FACT or FICTION

CHRIS GRABENSTEIN is the #1 *New York Times* bestselling author of *Escape from Mr. Lemoncello's Library, Mr. Lemoncello's Library Olympics, The Island of Dr. Libris,* the Welcome to Wonderland series, and many other books, as well as the coauthor of numerous fun and funny page-turners with James Patterson, including the I Funny, House of Robots, and Treasure Hunters series, *Word of Mouse,* and *Jacky Ha-Ha.* Chris grew up going to St. Petersburg, Florida, every summer and loved visiting roadside attractions like Gatorland, the fabulous Tiki Gardens, Weeki Wachee Springs, and the "talking mermaids" at Webb's City. Chris lives in New York City with his wife, J.J. You can visit Chris at ChrisGrabenstein.com. And look for his next book, *Mr. Lemoncello's Great Library Race,* coming soon!

BROOKE ALLEN graduated from Savannah College of Art and Design and is the illustrator of the critically acclaimed, Eisner Award–winning *Lumberjanes.*